MICHAEL HEATH

The Anger of My Heart

"My tongue will tell the anger of my heart, or else my heart concealing it will break."

William Shakespeare
The Taming of the Shrew

Contents

1

A VACANCY IS FILLED

It was an egg stain. As obvious as if it had been in the centre of her forehead. And what was so maddening was that the distinctive colour of her duck egg blue dress was the perfect backdrop to accentuate its greasy glow. A glance to the door reassured her that the butler had not yet re-entered the room, so she scratched quickly at the offending smear and removed as much of the residue as she could. A creak of floorboard outside the room caused her to momentarily stiffen and she affected to look nonchalantly towards a large bookcase. But, thankfully, the door in the corner remained firmly closed and, confident now that no one was about to enter, she immediately employed the nail of her index finger to worry away at the stain once more.

The room that she had been shown into was the library of Grove Hall; it was lit by one large window at the far end, light pouring through to brighten the burgundy walls. An elaborate cornice connected wall to ceiling and an immense chandelier was a suspended spray of glass that caught the colours and glints around it.

She stood up and walked over to a series of paintings which seemed to have been executed by the same artist. The pictures were various bucolic views which reminded her of her time in France when she had been working there. As she studied each painting in turn, she felt there was something odd about them but was at a loss as to what made her feel that way.

A bookcase ran along one side of the long wall and she inspected it with a finger lightly grazing various leathery bookends, as if drawing the knowledge of each tome through her fingerprint. So many of the books were guides to other countries: Spain, Italy, Austria, France...

Grove Hall itself was an impressive building said to date from the early 17th century, and originally a two-story building of red brick, before a third storey was added sometime in the early 19th century.

The house was set well back from the road that ran between Kenton and Ashfield, hidden from view by a high wall that fronted the lane and behind which had been planted beech, elm, and oak, all of which were now fully mature. Through these trees threaded the main carriageway which delivered the visitor to the main entrance of the house. At the rear of the estate could be found a series of stepped lawns, low walls and large flower beds that sloped away until they met a dense wood fringed with rhododendrons.

When she had walked the entire room, viewed every painting and mentally noted those books which had caught her eye, she returned to her seat and wearily pondered whether it had been a wise decision to have come to the house at all. What was she doing here? Why was she putting herself through this? Was the income from this appointment so important to her existence that she should abase herself by once more being at the beck and call of the gentry? Thinking she would wait no longer, she lunged for her bag, rose abruptly from the chair and left the room.

The butler, who was just crossing the hall immediately outside the room, stopped and looked quizzically at her. There was something of the military man about him, she thought, especially the way his head seemed to be sitting at the back of his shoulders. Having learned to communicate all inner emotions with only the slightest twitch of his lips, he looked on as if all such sudden exits from the house were a daily occurrence at Grove Hall.

"Are you lost, Madam?"

"No, are you?"

"I merely thought..."

"Oh, I don't think you ever consider your thoughts as 'merely'. I would assume that you think all your thoughts as rather quite considerable. I will not wait any longer. Good day."

The woman had just reached the large pair of front doors to the house when she heard a voice from behind. "Please don't leave, Miss Smy. I apologise profusely for keeping you. You have every right to feel upset."

It was an absurd thing, but when Miss Smy turned and registered just who it was that had emerged from a neighbouring room to speak with her, she noticed that all three - herself, the butler and the woman who had called to her - were standing in a perfect triangle in the capacious hallway.

"Mrs Balthasar?"

"I would be most grateful if you would stay for a little longer. Cavenham, tell Berthe to bring us a tray of tea. Oh, Miss Smy, I trust that tea would be agreeable to you?" She pushed back a door and beckoned Miss Smy to re-enter the room she had just been waiting in.

"Thank you. Tea would be most refreshing."

Mrs Véronique Balthasar, with hands clasped in front of her, followed Winifred Smy into the room. "I always receive visitors in this room. The people from whom we've leased the house referred to it as the library, but I would hazard that they purchased their books by the yard rather than by applying any benchmark of quality."

"It's still very beautiful. Those paintings on the wall intrigued me..."

"Oh, they're just some pictures of our own which we hung, just to make it feel more like home. Now, Miss Smy, I am extremely grateful that you have spared me a little of your time. I know that my punctuality has been extremely remiss, but I can assure you that the cause was not within my control."

Miss Smy found herself directed back to the small divan and arranged herself so that her arm would hide the egg stain on her dress. Mrs Balthasar moved across the room with the easy air of one who felt themselves to be a model of taste and deportment. She took a seat on the opposite divan, sitting sideways as if posing for some secreted photographer.

There was no doubt, thought Winifred Smy, that Mrs Balthasar was a fine-looking woman. She estimated her age to be probably in her late thirties yet her skin was fresh and her figure seemingly untroubled by any first rounding out of early middle age. But there was something about her eyes, a tender sadness that emanated from them, even when she smiled.

"It was good of you to speak with me today. Mr Pilbeam, whom I met recently, reassures me of your excellent character. I understand that your parents are now dead. Your father was in the army?"

"Yes. He died in the second Afghan war."

"In battle?"

"Apparently so. My mother received a letter from his commanding officer to that effect."

Mrs Balthasar adjusted the folds of her dress whilst Miss Smy spoke.

"And your mother?" She asked the question with eyes now averted to the adjustment of a small bracelet.

"She died two years ago. Her health was never very strong, especially towards the end."

"How interesting."

Miss Smy, irritated at the patronising tone of Mrs Balthasar, responded sharply. "There was nothing 'interesting' about the nature of my mother's health."

"Yes, oh yes, quite. Most distressing."

Miss Smy became aware that she was speaking with that class of person who, because they are wealthy and blessed with an overwhelming conviction of their own superiority, often ignore the conversation of those they deem below their station. Yes, they affect to engage in small talk but seldom listen to what is said, unless it is news that imperils the important events and activities of their own lives.

"A recent acquaintance of mine, Mrs Chevallier, tells me that you were previously a governess some years ago in London. She also communicated that you were well-favoured but inclined to leave at very short notice."

"Mrs Chevallier and I are well known to each other, and I would suggest that she has a higher opinion of my character than to imply that there was little reason for my departure. I had received word that my mother was very ill. I asked the master of the house, Lord Kenilworth, if I might immediately resign and tend to her. He acceded to my request, and I left in good favour. When it comes to those I love dearest, my loyalty to them will always come first."

"I see, Miss Smy. Perhaps we might turn to the business in hand? I would like to relate the reasons as to why I have asked you here today. Some time ago, two labouring people known well to my father asked if I would honour them by being the godmother to their only child, a young girl called Melka. As they were good people and held in high esteem by my father, I reluctantly acquiesced and agreed to their invitation."

A ticklish cough began to rise in Winifred Smy's throat and she lifted her hand to cover her mouth. Realising now that the egg stain was in full view she found herself caught in an embarrassing choreography of moving her left arm over to cover the stain, whilst her right hand muted the impact of her cough. Mrs Balthasar pretended not to notice but Miss Smy was fully aware that she had.

"Of course, that christening was some eleven years ago or so, and now they have approached me with another most unorthodox request. I hesitate to reveal that request to you and, before I do, would seek reassurance of the highest degree of confidence on your part. Tell me, is my confidence well placed?"

Miss Smy was irritated with the fact that Mrs Balthasar should need to ask but, as she was still trying to stifle her cough, chose instead to nod her acquiescence. Clearing her throat, she was at last able to answer. "If the question that you really want to ask me is will I betray any confidence that you may wish to share, then the answer is most resolutely, no."

"My godchild, Melka Eary, has been raised in a deeply rural

community which lacks many of the opportunities that one might associate with a more cultured and refined upbringing. Her education has been - how do I put this? - rudimentary, and they have asked that she might continue her studies in our home. I spoke with my husband on this very matter and he was most persuasive and supportive that I should accept their request, encouraging me with great energy that my goddaughter should place herself under my wing."

"And so she is to join you here at Grove Hall?"

"Melka is here already. Her...that is Mr and Mrs Eary, delivered her on Saturday to us. And a most difficult hour it was to bear."

"Why difficult?"

"Have you no imagination, Miss Smy? How must the poor child have felt to be passed over to me? A godmother she had never met who has lived for the most part in Europe. Whatever superior gifts and education I might put before her will not compensate for the loss of the love and company of those who have raised her."

"But that sounds as if Melka's staying with you is now a permanent arrangement. Is that what you are really saying?"

Mrs Balthasar stood up and moved to the broad window. "Miss Smy, I must confess that I find your manner most direct. Direct to the point of impertinence. Indeed, it raises doubts within me that you would be the right person for this appointment."

"Then you must find someone who is much more in keeping with your expectations. I will respect any decision on your part and be quite happy to give way to somebody more suitable to you."

Mrs Balthasar turned sharply and confronted Miss Smy, "You

seem to imply that Melka is not someone you would be willing to help?”

“On the contrary, I feel that my influence on Miss Melka would be such that you wouldn't wish to engage me.”

The awkwardness between both was as brittle and sharp as a shaft of sunshine draped across a stone floor. After some time, Mrs Balthasar spoke. “I think your influence on my godchild would prove difficult. She has been through much heartache, and I am unconvinced that your presence would ease her situation.”

“You are probably right. If she were to pass to my tutelage, I would teach her some of my most dreadful convictions. Awful and abhorrent ideas such as she is the equal of, and often superior to, the very men who patronise her. That she has the right to expect so much more than the claustrophobic and destructive notion that she spends the rest of her life in the service of some vastly inferior male. That she has the right to choose not to marry - or if she does - that it would be a decision that she took of her own choosing and quite uncorrupted by the scheming machinations of overweening godparents.”

“How dare you! How dare you air your views so brazenly in my house!”

Not for the first time that morning, Miss Smy stood up, gathered her few belongings and made to leave. “I must bid you good day, Mrs Balthasar. I am incapable of being anything other than myself. Thank you for the kind offer of some tea. I am sure it would have been delightful.”

But Mrs Balthasar didn't answer. Instead, she sat once more on her sofa, joined her two hands on her lap and breezily inquired, “When can you start Miss Smy?”

2

COMPANY FOR MISS SMY

"I have a bit of news. I am employed again."

The information was enough to cause Gladys Cupper to halt her removal of some tired carnations from the vase and turn towards Miss Smy, her eyes wide with surprise. "But I thought you'd no need to work? Mr Cupper told me that you were set up good 'n' proper for the rest of your days."

"So I am, and to be perfectly frank, I was quite settled with the idea that I would never work again. And then a letter arrived from a Mrs Balthasar asking me to meet her. She had a proposition she wanted to put to me."

"A proposition? What she wanten then?"

"That I would be a governess for her goddaughter."

"Her goddaughter? She's a mite too uppity that woman is. If you have to go back to work, surely tha's better folk who would employ yew. Anyway, why yew worken again? You still haven't told me."

Winifred Smy rose from her seat and passed a large jug of water to Gladys. "Oh, I need to be using my brain again. Break out of this routine I've got into. Get out of bed, read, have breakfast, go into Debenham, come home, lunch, tea, and so on. This seemed like the perfect answer, although I agree with you about Mrs Balthasar. She's uppity indeed."

With the flowers artfully ordered in the vase, Gladys Cupper took the jug and poured the fresh water in before stepping back to reassure herself that they were to her satisfaction.

"So how did she find out about yew, Fred?"

"Apparently, she asked the Reverend Pilbeam if there was someone local who might be suitable. It was he who recommended me. Then she took a sort of reference from Mrs Chevallier."

"Well, good luck 's all I'll say. And I don't care for her husband either. He's a German."

"Austrian apparently, not German. Made his money in banking, I understand, and a lot of it from what I hear."

Gladys Cupper wiped her hands on her pinafore, took one last glance at the flowers before returning to the kitchen table. "Well, if this war gets goin', he'll be as good as German as far as I'm concerned. Hasn't he already got a child of his own? A son I wuz told."

"Augustus. Rather full of himself I think. I reckon 'like stepmother like son'. I met him as I was leaving. Cavenham, their butler, had just ushered me out of the house as our Mr Augustus was dismounting from his horse. I wished him a 'Good morning' and he stared in the most obnoxious manner. He's only fifteen or sixteen years old but seemed a rather supercilious young man."

"You've hardly touched your cake, Fred."

"Oh, I've no appetite this morning, Glad. You know my funny ways. Let me take it with me and I'll finish it when I'm hungry. There is no finer baker of cakes - or bread for that matter - than you and I would rather have it when I'm ready to enjoy it."

"Here, dew yew let me wrap a couple of slices up for yew before you go. And I've baked just the loveliest biscuits yesterday mornen. My John has already been eaten too many of 'em, big-bellied man that he is."

With Gladys Cupper's cake safely in her bag, Winifred Smy took the Kenton Road towards Debenham that July morning, but as she neared the corner where the lane passed Pages Farm, she caught the briefest glimpse of a man who had quickly withdrawn behind one of the barns. She thought no more of it until she reached the row of small cottages that stood beside the windmill. Glancing suddenly behind her, she thought she briefly saw the same man dart behind a large hedge. She was sure that, whoever this man was, he was not someone she knew. Refusing to be unnerved by this sinister presence, she quickened her pace and took the field path that linked the windmill to the village of Debenham.

There had been a light shower but, after the long days of dry weather, all traces of the rain had long dried out. Upon reaching the High Street in Debenham she was glad to spot Mrs Corner who was crossing the road from Gracechurch Street.

"Oh, Mrs Corner! Mrs Corner!"

"Good day to you, Miss Smy. Shoppen?" Mrs Corner was medium in so many ways. She was of medium height and weight. She had never been the brightest child in her class but was never the dullest either. She had occasional moments of perception when in conversation with others and many moments when she looked dreamy and disconnected from those around her. But if there was one feature that was truly exceptional about her, it was that she had the palest grey eyes that Winifred Smy had ever seen. Not the grey of cold slate but the pale grey of a benign raincloud.

"Yes, a few things to get while I'm here. I'm really glad I met you; I wanted to ask if Spadger Peck had been in The Dove lately?"

Mrs Corner rolled those greyest of eyes and grimaced. "Not lately. In fact, I carn't remember now if he's been barred or not, so often I 'ave to do it. Why yew asken? He dussent owe yew money, I 'ope?"

"Not at all. I just need to ask a favour of him. Here…" Miss Smy reached into her bag for her purse. "Put these few coins behind the bar for him and ask him to drop by if he's passing through Kenton. That's if you'll have him back in the pub, of course."

Mrs Corner smiled resignedly and shook her head. "He's an old rapscallion, is that Spadger. Of course, I'll tell 'im. Can I ask what fer?"

"Because when you think you're being trailed by a fox, it's wise to have the finest poacher in Suffolk trailing the fox."

3

GASPARD'S GRAVE WALK

The grave was now tidied and Winifred Smy stood up and stretched her aching limbs. Her hands were dirty and the cold mud had burrowed its way beneath her nails and imprinted itself on her fingertips. She recalled how her mother had always insisted that she should be buried at the edge of the churchyard, as if the placing of the grave might convey to the innocent onlooker that she was reluctant to be interred there and would rather cross the boundary of 'God's acre' and be back amongst the living.

"You know, I always ask myself why people build walls around a churchyard; the dead can't escape and the living have no desire to take up residence."

Winifred Smy looked up to see a middle-aged man, unnaturally handsome and with a self-assurance that only those who are irrefutably certain of their masculine appeal to others always possess. In his right hand he held an ebony walking stick with a distinctive hatch-carved shaft. Winifred Smy suspected that such a stick would never be used for support, only for show. She also detected something of the roué about him, although his smooth face betrayed no visible signs of a misspent life.

"French, Monsieur?"

"French, Madame."

"Mademoiselle."

The man bowed but couldn't fail to express his surprise. "Mademoiselle? My apologies. Your mother?" He pointed - rather disrespectfully Smy thought - at the headstone with his cane.

"My mother. Are you staying locally?"

"Kenton Hall. Colonel Capon has been most accommodating. This morning I felt the sudden need to have a little walk and clear the senses."

"Un peu d'air frais?"

"Well, an English person speaking excellent French! I am impressed, Mademoiselle. As I was saying, I decided to take a little exercise and so I followed a path back there," again his cane directed the attention of Miss Smy. "And this is where it has led me. And these surroundings - and your bewitching presence - are a delightful discovery I was not expecting."

Winifred Smy brushed her hands together and tried not to feel too uncomfortable under the stranger's gaze.

"Will you be walking back the way you came?"

The man's demeanour changed immediately. "That would depend. If you were walking along the same path, then that would emphatically be the path for me."

Smy now folded her arms and smiled. "Then you are destined to walk alone. I have an aversion to clumsy overtures."

"Pardon, Mademoiselle?"

"Ne m'insultez pas avec vos manières, monsieur."

"Ah, a woman with spirit! Once more I must apologise. Please, allow me to introduce myself. My name is Marc-Antoine

Gaspard. I truly meant no offence."

What was it about him that was so striking? Miss Smy did not fail to notice the slimness of his physique but imagined it as a toned slimness rather than any sort of weak physicality. His clothes were a mixture of the conventional and the maverick, wearing a suit of the sternest grey but with a mustard waistcoat which was a bold statement of confident originality. Yet all this was a sideshow to the undeniable attractiveness of his features. Miss Smy was almost resentful to accept that he was beautifully handsome.

"My name is Winifred Smy, Monsieur Gaspard. Do you always gravitate towards graveyards when walking?"

Marc-Antoine Gaspard chose not to answer. He put the silver embossed tip of his cane on the ground and looked up at the church. "Interesting building. That is a chantry chapel, if I am not mistaken."

"The Garneys. Lords of the manor. They owned much of the land around here at one time. That grave next to the church wall houses one of them." Smy nodded towards a pale limestone chest tomb standing against the chancel wall. "It was they who commissioned the chapel."

"Interesting. This man Garney seems to have loved his chapel so much that he was buried next to it?"

"Oh, it was the custom in England at one time that the more elevated you were in the parish, the closer to the church you were buried."

"And I am sure that the priest's daily prayers secured an immediate entry into God's holy kingdom for Monsieur Garney."

Winfred Smy smiled wryly but chose to change the subject. "I presume that Colonel Capon must be an old friend?"

"Why, yes. Very much so. Do you mind if I refresh myself?"

Gaspard reached inside his jacket and took out a beautiful silver and glass hip flask, from which he drank what Miss Smy estimated to be most of its contents. "My apologies, but it helps to remove the aftertaste of your interesting English breakfast."

Winifred Smy picked up the cloths that she had used to clean her mother's headstone. "I must be on my way, Monsieur. I have an appointment to keep."

"Are you walking past Kenton Hall, perhaps?"

"No, I am going to cycle to Grove Hall. It's quicker for me to take the Low Road."

"Ah, Grove Hall. I think I've heard of it. Herr Balthasar?"

Miss Smy was taken aback by the fact that, for one that had so recently arrived in the area, Gaspard should know the occupants of a house in a neighbouring village.

"You are acquainted with Herr Balthasar?"

"Oh, Colonel Capon mentioned him last night at dinner. Something about Balthasar and banking, but he speaks very fast. I consider my English as normally quite sufficient for most situations, but the Colonel often loses me here and there. Now, I am delaying you and, reluctantly, I must let you continue with your day."

"Is your stay with Colonel Capon a short one?"

"Oh, the Colonel has been most gracious because I am not sure how long I will encumber him, but I would expect to return to France very soon. You live nearby, mademoiselle?"

"I do. I must wish you good day, Monsieur."

Gaspard, who was returning the now near-empty flask to his pocket, bowed his head slightly and gave Miss Smy the most enigmatic smile. As she walked down the churchyard path she could sense that Marc-Antoine Gaspard had remained where she had left him. Returning to her cottage on the opposite side of the road from the church, she waited a few moments before picking up a shallow basket in her kitchen and walking into her back garden, nonchalantly looking across the road, intrigued to see if Monsieur Gaspard was still there. He wasn't and she continued to walk around the perimeter of her garden, taking pleasure at the swelling fruit of her pear trees and delighting in the comforting warmth of the sun.

The singularity of that morning's encounter in the churchyard continued to nag away as she prepared herself for the cycle ride to Grove Hall. There was an oddness about Monsieur Gaspard's presence that she couldn't fathom. Was it just coincidence that had brought them together that morning? Or was there more than mere serendipity to their meeting?

As she rode along Low Road towards the village of Ashfield, she found that these ruminating thoughts stayed with her until she happened to glance at a footpath that bisected one of the fields that rose to her right. There, quite distinctly, was a man some 300 metres or so away from her. Too far away for her to discern his features, but close enough to see that he walked with a distinct limp. Winfred Smy was well acquainted with all of the farmers and labourers of the parish, and she now had no doubt that this was someone she had never seen before. Realising that the stranger was the same man who had shadowed her on her walk to Debenham, she experienced a sudden alarm which brought a panicked edge to the speed of her cycling.

She glanced back once more and saw that he was trying to run down the path towards the road, but that his afflicted leg prevented him from being able to achieve any speed.

She had yet to reach Grove Hall but found herself unnerved by the two encounters that morning: Marc-Antoine Gaspard and the limping man. What troubled her most of all was that her determinedly rational turn of mind resolutely refused to provide her with answers. And Miss Smy always obsessed over a need for answers.

4

THE SILENCE IS SHATTERED

When Winifred Smy entered the room she was immediately confronted with the hostile stare of Mrs Balthasar. "You are late, Miss Smy."

"I am not late. You are early, Mrs Balthasar. The time is not yet ten o'clock. The very beautiful Grandfather clock in your entrance hall verifies my time of arrival does it not?"

On the floor at the far end of the room sat Melka, her back resolutely turned against the adults who were annoyedly sparring behind her.

"Melka! Melka! Come here, child."

But Melka did not move. The window that she sat by had been slightly opened by one of the servants, and the heavy curtains received and absorbed the small gusts of wind that blew in from the garden.

Winifred Smy bent slightly forward and discreetly suggested, "I think that your goddaughter and I would be better left alone. Please trust my experience in dealing with this situation."

Mrs Balthasar continued to look resentfully at Miss Smy but eventually agreed. After she had left the room, it struck Miss

Smy that she already felt only too ready to relinquish her new position and return the responsibility for dealing with Melka's intransigence back to Mrs Balthasar.

She walked up to the hunched figure of Melka and sat on a nearby chair. For several minutes they both stared through the broad sash window and watched two gardeners who were doggedly working through their various labours. The lightest of rain now began to fall, its feeble spats lazily resting on the glass.

"You do not want to be here, do you? And you are now sitting near someone you do not want to be with. But I would like to be with you, Melka. And I like this place where we are sitting together. I would also like to know you. I think I would like you to know me as well. I am sure that I am very old to you, but I think I am interesting nonetheless."

Winifred Smy moved from the chair by the window and sat on the floor, staring out at the ragged clouds that were being slowly evaporated by the afternoon sun. The green of the wide lawn looked vulnerable, the gardeners having just shaved its sward to such a shallow depth that it now looked scalped and defeated.

"Are you Miss Smy?"

"I am."

"Melka is a horrible name."

Winifred Smy looked at the tightened figure of the child, her thin limbs pulled into her frail body as if she desperately wanted to reduce her physical presence in the world.

"Oh, I think Melka a beautiful name. Which school have you been going to?"

"Clopton."

"Ah, that's near Grundisburgh, isn't it? Do you like it?"

"No. I don't loike the teacher. She's too strict. Are yew strict?"

"You must tell me. Do I look strict?"

"Yes."

"Then I suppose I must be. But I don't think I am." Winifred Smy stood up and held out both hands to Melka. "Would you like to come with me? You'll find I don't bite."

A small room on the top floor had been set aside as a classroom. When they both entered, Smy moved the writing desk to one side so that only two chairs remained in the centre. She had also brought a few wildflowers and placed them in a small vase by the window.

Over the course of the next few days, Melka began to relax and, without being prompted, intimated to Miss Smy that drawing was her favourite subject. Acting on this intelligence, Smy proposed that, on the last day of the week, they both take pencils and paper outside after they had had their lunch but with the caveat that it would only happen if enough progress was made with Melka's completion of some grammar and mathematical exercises. The prospect of Miss Smy's proposal brought an unmistakable zeal to Melka's studies and the early Friday afternoon saw them strolling down the long lawns behind Grove Hall, looking for a suitable position from which they could both sketch.

Eventually, they settled on a corner of the large garden and Miss Smy watched Melka as she immediately opened a page in her sketchbook before looking up to survey the view. How different Melka's manner now was. She seemed more confident, more assured. The frailty of her figure was transformed into a supple alertness and a hitherto cowering demeanour gave way to an attentive posture with shoulders thrown back as her eyes took in the gardens and imposing house before her. Miss Smy expected her to begin drawing but Melka looked resolutely forward, taking in each detail that sat before her. With unblinking eyes, she almost seemed to absorb the view, gathering in her brain every shadow, curve and angle. She registered the colour of the brick, the sunlight's sheen as it streaked across the slate roof, the way the light bounced back from the windows.

At first, thin lines were confidently traced onto Melka's paper, which Smy instantly recognised as the strong angles of the house bordered by the delicate curves of the elms and oaks that framed one side of it. Melka constantly moved her gaze from the page to the house and then back to the page. Her small hand brushed the pencil's point across the paper with the lightest of passing strokes. Magically, the scene before her began to assume its identical dimensions onto the sketchbook page, as Melka rendered what she could see with an uncanny accuracy. The pleasure of watching Melka's precocious talent caused Miss Smy to quite forget her own drawing and she eventually placed her sketchpad and pencils to one side so that she might continue to marvel at Melka's expertise.

As Melka drew, two warring blackbirds emerged from beneath a nearby hawthorn and skittered in short bursts of movement like two gladiators looking to make the first strike. A jay alighted on a high branch of a towering Scots Pine, only to quickly disappear again as if embarrassed by its showy plumage. At regular intervals, the warm arms of the sun's rays fell upon the wide lawns until another cloud fell across to dull its display.

Whenever Miss Smy recalled the events of the next few seconds, she remembered that they always seemed to merge into a single happening but knew that this was impossible.

Did the panicked screeching of the pheasant occur before or after the sound of the gunshot? It did not matter. What followed almost instantly was the emergence of a man from the rhododendrons that lay beneath the many conifers screening the very back of the garden. Although still some distance away, Smy could immediately see that he was in great distress, lurching pathetically forward onto the open lawn before his body crumpled and fell.

Miss Smy and Melka were momentarily stunned but soon discarded their sketching materials to run frantically across to where the man was now lying face down. Melka easily outpaced Miss Smy but slowed to a walking pace as she approached the man. Some nine or ten yards away from where he lay she slowly fell to her knees as if about to pray. She pressed her hands to her face and emitted the most primal howl of grief, one that seemed to occupy the entire landscape with its agony. She then rose clumsily, ran forward and threw herself across the man.

"Pa! Pa!"

5

CHURCH TIDINGS

The Reverend Pilbeam clutched the corners of the pulpit so hard that his knuckles were white. He was a man who loved the theatre of a Sunday sermon, and it was only the most exhausted of villagers who fell asleep as he harangued the congregation.

"So, also, is the resurrection of the dead." His arms relaxed and he eyed those who sat before him, all riveted by the dramatic pauses that he allowed to fall between each sentence with the conviction of a barrister who knows that the jury is in the palm of his hand.

"It is sown in corruption; it is raised in corruption; it is sown in dishonour; it is raised in glory."

He raised both hands with fingers spread like a magician, proving that there was nothing hidden up either, capacious sleeve. Interrupting the silence that rested easily in the nave, there came the chirruping of chicks from a late nest that had been built in a woodpile at the edge of the churchyard, the heat of the late morning having necessitated the opening of the door in the south porch.

"It is sown in weakness; it is raised in power; it is sown a natural body; it is raised a spiritual body." Pilbeam took a moment to steady himself, turning from the histrionic vocabulary of the King James Bible to the philosophy of an educated vicar whose duty it is to keep the Kenton parishioners on the narrow path to God's salvation.

"We may turn over in our minds the senseless death of Thomas Eary and find it hard to reconcile such a dreadful event with a loving God. But, dearest brethren, there is a plan and it is God's plan. And we cannot know God. We are part of that plan and, in God's own good time, we will come to understand His will."

Miss Smy was now regretting choosing to sit in the chantry chapel. The sun, although still gaining height in the sky, was now pouring the full force of its heat through the chapel's side windows.

Soon enough, though, the service was completed and the high and low of Kenton's population began to exit the church, strictly observing the hierarchical rules of egress through the south porch.

Miss Smy, refusing to take any position in the line that might reflect her own conception of her social status, turned in her pew to see how much of the queue had disappeared and the appropriate moment to rise from her seat and leave the church. Staring back at her from the opposite side of the nave was Marc-Antoine Gaspard, who slowly nodded, with an almost cherubic smile, his acknowledgement of her presence. His being in the last pew towards the back of the church meant that the low morning sun streamed through the door of the south porch, bathing him in its virginal glow.

Smy behaved as if she had not seen him and turned back to

look at the altar. She knew she was feeling the greatest sense of discomfort but was unable to rationalise exactly why. Yes, he was a striking-looking man. Yes, he was obviously learned and perceptive. But there was something uncomfortable about him. He unsettled her, and that annoyed her most of all. So, determined to exhibit a disinterested manner, she continued to concentrate her gaze on the simple chancel in front of her.

"A fine sermon, mademoiselle?"

Smy was shocked to receive this sentence from just over her left shoulder. Gaspard had, in those brief seconds, repositioned himself in the pew directly behind her. She half-turned her head, smiled, and then returned her eyes to the chancel.

Once more the voice behind her spoke. "This Reverend Pilbeam. He is more an actor than a priest, do you not think?"

"It's not my place to say. My religious convictions are so weak that I would rather direct your question to those whose faith has a sounder foundation. I come to church out of loyalty, not religious zeal."

His voice was at her ear again, Gaspard having leant forward behind her. "May I talk with you for a moment? I promise to be very agreeable to you in my conversation."

When both Smy and Gaspard walked out of the church it was to be met by the Reverend Pilbeam who smiled heartily at both, secretly glad that the torture of feigned conversations with the village hoi-polloi was complete.

"Ah, Miss Smy. It is always a pleasure to welcome the pagan to our religious community. By the way, I have this for you." Pilbeam reached beneath his cassock and withdrew a carefully folded piece of paper, which he handed to her. Miss Smy opened the paper and studied it for some moments, with her finger pressed to her lips.

"The Albin Counter Gambit. Interesting. Your middlegame will be all the more threatening, I fear. I will reply in my usual way. Oh, may I introduce Monsieur Gaspard to you? We met very briefly when I was tending my mother's grave. He is staying with Colonel Capon for a few weeks."

The height difference between the two men was so great that, when their hands joined in a handshake, they were level with Pilbeam's chest.

"A most enlightening sermon, Reverend. I had no idea that this poor man...what was his name?"

"Eary, Thomas Eary."

"Why yes, this Thomas Eary. Why was he hiding in the bushes like that?"

Winifred Smy turned quizzically to Gaspard and asked, "How do you know he was hiding in the bushes?"

"Well, people have been telling me..."

"How could they? The fact that Eary was dead has been confirmed by the police. But, according to Mr Balthasar, the circumstances of his death have not been communicated to anyone. You have obviously been talking to someone who is most knowledgeable in this matter."

"Mademoiselle, Colonel Capon himself had already told me that you have a fine mind and now you have demonstrated his high opinion of you so clearly to me. But I would remonstrate that you will be as aware as I am that these matters soon become the gossip of everyone around."

Smy could not help but notice Gaspard's complete and ir-refutable self-possession. When speaking to her his beautiful eyes had never wavered and he spoke with an unhurried tone that betrayed no feeling of discomfort.

Winifred Smy refused to be disoriented by Gaspard's easy

charm, coolly remarking, "Indeed, in these parts, rumour and gossip moves with a rapidity that has never failed to impress me. But even many of those who work at Grove Hall have been shielded from the events of that day. So, if you have no objection to me asking, who told you about where poor Mr Eary was when he died?"

Gaspard took out his watch from his waistcoat. "I am late for my appointment! Miss Smy, you will forgive me I know. But I have a meeting that I dare not be late for. *À bientôt.*"

With another slight bow, he walked briskly away. Smy watched him leave the churchyard, her mind unsettled by the conversation. Why, as he had mentioned in the church not ten minutes ago, had he wanted to talk with her? And why, after the uncomfortable exchange between them about the source of his information, did he leave so suddenly?

"A most peculiar man, according to Colonel Capon." It was the voice of the Reverend Pilbeam that interrupted her thoughts.

"He certainly is. I know nothing of him. I met him for the first time this week and he mentioned that he was staying at Kenton Hall. Yes, a most peculiar man."

"Do you know what I found extremely fascinating about him?"

"Tell me."

"All through the morning's service he constantly looked at the church door as if he was expecting someone to arrive. When old Johnson came in late, he looked sorely disappointed. Now why was that I wonder?"

"I'm sure there's a good reason. Oh, my dear Mister Pilbeam. I have just realised that, as we were watching Monsieur Gaspard leave just now, something was missing."

6

CALLS AN INSPECTOR

"Good morning, Inspector."

Inspector Tranmer, who had been sitting in the very same seat that Smy herself had occupied on her first visit to Grove Hall, rose to greet her.

"Miss Smy. What a pleasant surprise!"

"How can it be a surprise? Cavenham informed me that you asked to see me by name."

Tranmer looked rather confused for a moment before resuming his professional manner.

"Please, do take a seat."

Winifred Smy lowered herself into the chair while her eyes remained fixed on the uncomfortable figure of Tranmer, who had dropped his pencil and was now retrieving it from beneath the skirt of the divan's covering. Steadying himself, he suddenly sat bolt upright in an attempt to look authoritative.

"How have you been, Inspector?"

"Quite well, Miss Smy. But do please call me Herbert. It is my name, as you know."

"I do know, but I also remember a conversation about the

division between your personal and professional life. This meeting is connected with your professional life, so I think the wiser protocol is to call you Inspector."

Tranmer's posture became more formal as he said with a theatrically lower voice, "Miss Smy, I have been interviewing all those employed or living in this house about the death of Mr Thomas Eary. I would..."

"Do you mean the murder of Thomas Eary?"

Tranmer looked momentarily irritated but decided to persevere. "I wish to talk to you about the *death* of Thomas Eary and would be enormously grateful if you could answer some questions."

"Enormously grateful, Inspector? Are there grades to your gratitude? Does the spectrum of your appreciation range from slightly grateful to enormously grateful?"

"Miss Smy, I would be most...grateful if you would just answer my questions."

"Of course. Are they your questions, or questions that someone has recommended you ask me?"

Tranmer visibly grew more confident and sat back on the sofa. "My questions, Miss Smy."

"Ask away, Herbert."

"Inspector."

"Oh, I thought you just told me that your name was Herbert."

Tranmer leapt from the sofa and said in a raised voice, "Please do not play games, Miss Smy! This is a very awkward moment for me. I did not choose to meet with you about this but I was told I had no choice."

"Do you know that your Yorkshire accent becomes much more pronounced when you are angry, Inspector?"

Tranmer stared at Smy and, with a steady delivery that took

even Winfred Smy by surprise, he replied, "But at least it is an accent that tells you where I am from, rather than an accent that disguises who I really am."

Winifred Smy betrayed no emotion and yet it was obvious that Tranmer's reply had found its mark. With a softer voice, she said, "I will not respond to that retort. To do so would be to grant it a dignity it does not deserve."

Tranmer walked to the corner of the room and gathered his thoughts. Smy relaxed and scrutinised him carefully as he buttoned up his suit jacket. He then turned and sat down once more on the divan.

"Miss Smy, you are a key witness to the events on Friday. As you would expect, I must ask you some questions about what you saw. Miss Eary has described the dreadful events in some detail, but I know - through past experience - that your evidence would be helpful."

"I am not sure that I can add anything to what Melka has already told you."

"She said that you were both at the far end of the lawn but still some distance from the trees. Would you mind if we walked to that place and you talked me through what you saw that day?"

Smy and Tranmer strode across the lawn but, unlike the last time when she had walked the very same path with Melka, the grey bellies of huge clouds were now being dragged across the sky.

"Here we are again, Inspector, with a new murder to solve. I suspect that Suffolk keeps you much busier than you might have first anticipated?"

"I have a great regard for your intercession on the last two cases that we worked on, but this is very different. With this death…"

"I am convinced it is murder. How fascinating that you still cannot see the wood for the trees."

"If I might continue, Miss Smy, you are an important witness to this accident and it would be highly improper were you to start involving yourself in any of the informed suppositions concerning it."

"I seem to recall a similar request from you twice before. And yet on both occasions it was my involvement that led to results that you would never have achieved without my help. Ah, this is where Melka and I were sitting."

Tranmer was glad of the distraction and surveyed the area of lawn as if it would yield a vital clue in the investigation.

"Exactly who was sitting where?"

"I was here, and Melka just there." Smy indicated both spots with a casual wave of her arm.

"And what happened immediately before you became aware of Mr Eary?"

"I was watching Melka as she was drawing the main house and then there was a gunshot that caused us both to look behind. That was when Mr Eary came out from the trees and then fell to the ground. Oh no, Inspector. Oh dear God, no."

"Is something wrong, Miss Smy?"

Miss Smy walked away with the tips of her fingers pressed to her temples. She walked around for a few seconds as if desperately trying to recall something before turning towards the Inspector with a confused look on her face.

"Do you know, I'm not sure."

"Not sure about what?"

"This might be a trifling thing, but I can't tell you whether the gunshot came first and then Mr Eary emerged from the trees, or whether he was shot after he ran out from those rhododendrons."

"I think that's all rather academic."

"Oh no, Inspector. I think that may well be the clue that will finally convince you it was murder."

7

CANDLES AND CONTRADICTIONS

George and Molly Elwood were never to know that the villagers of Kenton slyly referred to them as 'the Hellwoods'. Some years ago one of them was found *in flagrante delicto* by the other; who the betrayer and betrayed were had never been revealed, but the upshot was that, since that day twenty-four years ago, they had never spoken directly to one another. When entering a shop they appeared to be two entirely unrelated people, but if any transaction was undertaken they would stand at the counter using the unhappy shopkeeper as a 'go-between' in their communications.

It was in Abbotts' store, on Chancery Lane that ran parallel to Debenham's High Street, that Winifred Smy met them both, having called in to buy some candles.

"Good morning, Miss Smy. Are you well?"

"Very well, thank you, Mrs Elwood. And how are you both?"

"I am happy enough. Perhaps Mr George might tell you how he is feeling today."

George Elwood possessed a face that was so flat, one might almost imagine it to have been shaped by an amateur potter. His eyes, set well back in his pudgy face, sparkled like the reflection of the overhead sun in a deep well.

"And how are you, Mr Elwood?"

"Hmm? I am very well, Miss Smy; thank you for asking. It's good to see you. Actually, it is rather a coincidence my meeting you here. You see, I understand that Mrs Elwood has something that she would like to ask you. If I were you, I would inquire as to whether she has any questions."

Winifred Smy, turned to Molly Elwood. "I understand you have something you'd like to ask, Mrs Elwood."

"However did you know, because I do indeed have a question. I have heard the terrible news about poor Thomas Eary. But I wanted to enquire as to what will become of his daughter? I heard from Mrs Cupper that she is staying with those people that moved into Grove Hall a short while ago. What's their name again?"

"Balthasar. Mr and Mrs Balthasar. The Earys asked if Mrs Balthasar might take Melka under their wing, so to speak. And, being the godmother, she has agreed to do that."

"Godmother? Mrs Balthasar? That's not right. She were never Melka's godmother. It was old Mrs Everson who stood godmother for her. I may not have seen Mrs Eary or Mrs Everson for many a month, but I was there on the day that that baby was baptised and can swear on the good book it were Mrs Everson, not no Mrs Balthasar."

"Are you sure?"

"Perhaps I could ask you to ask Mr Elwood. He will vouch for me, I am certain."

"Mr Elwood."

"Yes, Miss Smy?"

Smy, irritated by the idiocy of their communication, nevertheless decided to persevere. "Your wife tells me that Mrs Balthasar was not the godmother of Melka Eary, and that it is Mrs Everson. Is that true?"

"It's true. And a good friend to the Earys old Mrs Everson was. A real godmother to that girl in every way. She married a right slummock, but she were still a good'n."

When Smy found herself outside Abbotts' shop, having eventually extricated herself from the exasperating company of the Elwoods, she found that she had been quite taken aback. Who was she to believe? Yes, Mr and Mrs Elwood were a curious pair, but they did not have a reputation for peddling false gossip. But surely her new employer, Mrs Balthsar, had no reason to lie? In light of the recent death of Thomas Eary, these confusing and contradictory pieces of information seemed to hold some secret significance.

"Miss Smy?"

Winifred Smy looked around to see the broad smile of Spadger Peck looking back at her. "Oh, Spadger, I'm glad it's you."

"How yew diddlun?"

"Not so bad. Yourself?"

"Fair to middlen. Old Mrs Corner said you wanted to see me. You did me a favour there bein' as how she'd not been speaken to me since a month ago or so. Things goo crotchet with us roight now."

"So you've parted company with the Dove again, Spadger?"

"Ah, Mrs Corner is a bit botty, but we always come to an understanden. So, why you want to see me? Allus happy to help."

"Tell me, have you noticed anyone new in the parish these last few days? Maybe when you've been out on your travels."

Spadger took off his hat and tapped its brim on his chest as he thought. "Well, I've been abroad a good bit lately, so can't say I have. Why'd yew ask?"

"I just have this feeling. Perhaps an intuition. I really felt the other morning, when I was walking past Pages Farm, that I was being followed. I looked back but this figure just disappeared into the hedge. And then, only yesterday, as I was cycling to work at Grove Hall, the same man was running down a field path towards me. To be honest, Spadger, it unsettled me a good deal, especially as there was no one else around. So I thought it better to get away. He had a limp. A bad one from what I could see."

"Pages Farm, eh? Well I know one or two there, roight enough. One of 'em drinks in the Woolpack. Let me 'ave a word. A bad business up at Grove 'all. I dussent know yew were worken there. A tidy lot of pheasant used to be had on that land, but it's not as good as it was. I hear the marster there is a crack shot. Nice gun as well. Well, so I'm told that is, but yew know me, Miss Smy. I like to be abed when the sun's down."

Miss Smy said nothing but smiled knowingly at Spadger Peck. Spadger's nocturnal comings and goings were the worst kept secret in Debenham; even PC Cornish was known to turn a 'blind eye' to his unconventional hours of activity. One never knew for certain, but the sudden appearance of an occasional hare or partridge on Cornish's doorstep from time to time was often interpreted as the reward for his silence.

"I suppose you've heard about what happened recently at Grove Hall?"

"I did an' I 'eard it wuz an accident. Sounds a bit rum that. Tommy Eary wuz a good man. Knew 'im a little and 'is missus too. A Clopton man if I remember roight. 'Is own gun, I 'eard. That don't sit roight with me. 'E wuz allus as careful as careful could be. Carn't think why 'e wuz creepen round Grove 'all, though. Bit off 'is normal patch."

Smy decided that it would be indiscreet to respond to Spadger's comments and they soon parted by the post office. With her tasks now completed in Debenham, she decided that it would be best to head for home and walked back to the large church at the top of the rise that crested the High Street. Sure enough, there was her bike and she spent some moments deciding what was the best way to arrange her shopping bag before mounting it. A path passed diagonally across the churchyard of St Mary's, and she rode along it down to the gap between the two cottages that led out onto Cross Green.

As she drew level with the wall that stood between the cottages and the graveyard, she became aware that a man had stepped out from behind it with a raised arm. In her confusion, she lost balance on the bicycle and fell awkwardly onto the track, her head receiving a sharp blow from the wall as she toppled to the ground. She sensed an overwhelming swirl of dizziness and tried to open her eyes. A man – she was too dazed to notice any features – was standing over her. That was the last thing she remembered before she finally lost consciousness.

8

A REPRIEVE FOR MANNERS?

"**M**anners!"

So shocked was Manners by Miss Smy's angry recognition that he lurched backwards and hit his head on the same wall that had dazed Smy. She had been concussed for a minute or two, and consciousness returned slowly before her eyelids flickered and opened. There, bent over her, was Manners, whose facial features were rapidly twitching and contorting, expressing a dizzying number of emotions all falling between the two extremes of despair and relief.

"Miss Smy, I am so sorry." He was feeling for his fallen hat with one hand whilst his other vigorously rubbed the back of his head. "I am so dreadfully sorry."

Winifred Smy, who was now sitting up and brushing the dust from her own hat was infuriated. "What the devil were you doing, jumping out on me like that?"

"I didn't mean to. I had just come through the churchyard gate here and saw a cyclist coming down the path at some speed, so thought I would take refuge behind this wall until they'd passed. I had absolutely no idea it was you, believe me. When I

39

glanced around the wall to see how close you were you'd drawn quite level to me, took the most enormous fright and fell. Please, please let me help you up."

"You'll do no such thing." Miss Smy stood up slowly and made sure that there were no after-effects from the fall.

"Perhaps you might sit down in the church. I'll fetch you a glass of water."

"Stop fussing, Mr Manners. I am quite all right."

"Were you cycling back to Kenton? If you were, might I entreat you instead to walk a little of the way with me? I'm in a bit of a spot, you see."

Manners' openness took Smy a little by surprise. "Bit of a spot? You? What do you mean?"

Manners looked furtively around him like a mime artist checking for interlopers. All of Manners' movements were largely exaggerated, reminding Miss Smy of those silent film actors that she had seen several years ago in London. "Perhaps it's best not to talk here, Miss Smy."

Winifred Smy looked incredulously around at the serried rows of gravestones that stood in sleepy attention. "Surely there is no better place than this? After all, who are the dead going to tell your secret to?"

Manners walked in a small circle on the path considering the wisdom of Miss Smy's observation before emphatically nodding his agreement. "You're right. We do seem to be quite alone. Well, it's my editor."

"Your editor? I don't follow."

"You see, you'll remember that we worked together on that unfortunate murder of that magician's assistant. The one in Ipswich. Miss...Miss..."

"Her name was Martha Ludbrook. Yes, I remember."

"Well, that little exclusive raised my standing in the *Framlingham Weekly News* to a very high degree. Quite the chosen one, I was. And so I remained until two weeks ago when I unearthed a little thing about an altercation on the bowling green of *The Ipswich and Suffolk Club*. One member had accused another of unsportsmanlike behaviour during a tense game, and a most unseemly fight ensued with no quarter given by either man."

"Please, Mr Manners, could we move to the interesting part of your story, if there is one."

"Miss Smy, hear me out! The upshot of all this is that one of the pugilists on the green that day was none other than my editor. He was appalled that I should have found out, and even more appalled that I was proposing it for inclusion in our venerable newspaper. So, I have fallen from a great height, Miss Smy. Lucifer's descent from heaven was but a step off the pavement to what I have suffered. 'Farewell happy fields; Where joy forever dwells: Hail, horrors, hail.'"

"A Miltonic fall from grace, indeed," observed Winifred Smy archly, but Manners was too taken up with his own misery to notice the sarcasm.

"So I thought, what am I to do? How can I regain the esteem of my editor? And then this Eary story broke, which cheered me up no end because I knew this might be the very opportunity where I could re-establish my journalistic credentials once more. And then I had the most tremendous stroke of luck! I learned that a certain Miss Smy was present when this poor man died."

"How did you know I was there?"

"Miss Smy, a journalist of my reputation never reveals his sources. We have a commitment to acting with the highest integrity."

"I want to believe that you are being deliberately humorous,

Mr Manners, but I rather fear that you really believe what you are saying."

Manners removed his hat and placed it over his heart. "Honesty above all else, my dear Miss Smy."

Winifred Smy found herself lost for words with the utter self-delusion of Mr Manners. Yet she knew him of old, and was quite certain that he would enthusiastically sell his Mother to a Sheikh's harem if there was an exclusive story to be had.

"So how can I help you out of this 'spot' that you refer to?"

Manners looked around the churchyard once more, just in case any entrapped corpses had clambered out from their resting places to earwig what he would say next. In a lowered voice, he proposed, "We can help each other. We are a team. I was told officially that it was an accident, but I am no fool, I am certain it was not an accident. My storytelling antennae have never failed me and they are quivering and throbbing with the anticipation of a story just waiting to be discovered. Twice before I have come up with the goods. Robert Knight's killer in Kenton. Martha Ludbrook's killer in Ipswich. My track record is enviable indeed."

"I was under the misapprehension that it was I that unravelled these mysteries."

"Well, of course that's true. But did I not play my role in both escapades? Was I not a worthy foot soldier in those unravellings?"

Miss Smy could only be amazed by the utter impertinence of Nigel Manners. But she also sensed that this was indeed an opportunity and, after all, he was right: he could be terrier-like when there was information to be unearthed.

"Before I agree - and I still harbour reservations about reforming our 'team' as you put it - I'd like to ask you a question first. What do you know about the death of Mr Eary?"

"From what I understand, he was hiding in some bushes at the bottom of the large lawns at the rear of Grove Hall. Why he was hiding there, I do not know, but that was the first thing that struck me as most peculiar. He then sustained a gunshot which caused him to emerge from his hiding place and fall some ten or twenty yards onto the lawn. Apparently, his daughter and you were sketching a short distance away and she ran to him but he was already dead. That is what I know."

Miss Smy watched him carefully as he spoke and seemed reassured by the genuineness of his reply to her question.

"And what do you know of the reason why Melka was at Grove Hall?"

"If my source is to be believed, Mrs Balthasar had once stood as godmother for the Earys' daughter and they had asked her to, well, give the child an education that might change the direction of her life. Most noble of Mr and Mrs Balthasar to grant that request, I thought."

"Mr Manners, I have some rather disappointing news for you."

"Disappointing news? What disappointing news?"

"Even though I was indeed there on the fateful day, I'm afraid I only know what you know. I am not sure that I am really the person to get you out of your spot."

Manners looked utterly crestfallen. "How beastly. How terribly beastly."

"Ah," said Miss Smy, suddenly recalling a very recent conversation, "There's just one thing that you may not know."

Manners jerked himself upwards as if he were a puppet whose strings were connected to an unseen hand in the sky.

"Tell me, Miss Smy. For heaven's sake, give me a sign."

"I was just talking to the Elwoods not one hour ago, and Molly Elwood swore blind that Mrs Balthasar was not the godmother. So why would Mrs Balthasar tell me that she was?"

Manners' eyes creased with excitement. "Mrs Balthasar was not the godmother? Why would she claim that she was? And why was Thomas Eary hiding at the back of the garden that day? Oh, yes. It's a sign, Miss Smy. You have given me a sign!"

With his usual angular awkwardness, he ran up the church path that led back onto the High Street, trying to marshal the peculiar action of his thin legs as he did so. Then, almost at the gate, he turned and raised his hat to her and shouted. "It's a sign!"

9

A VISIT FROM BERTHE

Two weeks had now passed since the tragic event at Grove Hall. The awkward meeting with Inspector Tranmer, which had taken place on the following day, still played on Winifred Smy's mind. When had Mr Eary been shot? The received wisdom was that Mr Eary had accidentally shot himself first and then tumbled out of the bushes from where he'd been hiding. To others, especially the police, it was all very plausible, but she had noticed certain things that no one else had yet mentioned. Were they significant, or just factors that had no bearing at all on the matter?

She sat at her kitchen table and poured a second cup of tea for herself. What had the scene been like when she had revisited the same places - where they had been sketching and where Mr Eary had finally fallen - with Inspector Tranmer? Of course, there was nothing to see. It had even been difficult, despite the breezy confidence she had shown to the inspector when they were in the garden at Grove Hall, to exactly locate where she and Melka had been when those few minutes of the awful event had unfolded.

There were other questions that also preoccupied her. Why was Mr Eary hiding? And if, as she firmly believed, he had been murdered, why would anyone want to murder him? Melka spoke so lovingly of her 'Pa' that the impression that had been firmly fixed in Miss Smy's mind was of a man who was kindly and affectionate. There had obviously been a great bond between them and to have taken the decision to release her to the care of the Balthasars might have been one that haunted him daily. Perhaps that was the only reason he was in the bushes. Because he wished to reassure himself, from a discreet distance, that Melka was happy in her new situation. But then the question that instantly followed was how did he know that Melka and Miss Smy would be at that position in the garden that day? And why would he then be shot by an, as yet, unknown murderer? If he had been poaching, he would simply have been apprehended by either the gamekeeper or any of the serving staff that happened to be passing.

It was a sharp knock on her cottage door that diverted Miss Smy from her troubled musings. She opened the door to be met by the cold smile of Berthe, Mrs Balthasar's servant.

"Good morning, Miss Smy."

"Good morning, Berthe. Please come in."

Miss Smy pulled out a chair for Berthe to sit on, but the gesture was met with, "No, thank you. I won't be long. Mrs Balthasar has given me a message for you. Would you be so good as to go to meet with her at the house this afternoon at two o'clock?"

Berthe spoke perfect English with only a faint French accent to betray her nationality. But the words were delivered mechanically, as if it was a duty that she would prefer to have done with quickly.

"Of course. Would you like some tea?"

"It is kind of you to ask but, no, I must return. Mrs Balthasar has kindly permitted me the use of the car and the driver will be waiting."

Miss Smy followed Berthe outside. The children of Kenton were admiring with a sense of wonder the large Darracq that stood waiting for Berthe's return. However, the sense of awe had not stopped them running their small hands over the cream bodywork, much to the annoyance of the driver who repeatedly told them to keep away.

"How is your shoulder, by the way?"

"My shoulder? Why do you ask?"

"I noticed that it seems to be troubling you."

Berthe laughed, "An old injury, I'm afraid. I once fell off a horse and hurt my shoulder. It comes and goes. Good day, Miss Smy."

The Eye Road was too narrow to turn the car, so Miss Smy watched the driver head off towards Occold where, presumably, he might find a clear enough space to turn the car around. She looked at the children, still excited that such a thing of wonder should make its way into the ordinariness of their lives. Watching them reminded her of the singular, intense moments of her own childhood. The physical bustle and excitement of the Southwold Trinity Fair on South Green. The sand that scratched so pleasantly on the inside of her toes at Walberswick. The sight of her father as he brushed his boots in the back garden whilst the tunic of his army uniform hung on the kitchen door. Yes, in years to come, that stately Darracq would be a similarly indelible memory for these small children.

Once Miss Smy had left the village of Kenton behind on her way to her appointment that afternoon, it was with a certain trepidation that she cycled along the lanes to Grove Hall. But the mysterious limping man didn't reappear. Leaving her bike at the back of the house she walked around the building towards a side entrance, only to chance upon Augustus Balthasar who was leaning with his back against a wall.

"Good morning, Augustus."

"I think you meant to say, 'Good morning, Mister Augustus.'"

"I am of sound enough mind to know what I said and what I said will suffice perfectly."

As Miss Smy walked briskly past, he shouted, "I don't like common people in my house."

"No, nor do I," replied Miss Smy airily.

As Miss Smy walked into the kitchen she was met by Cavenham, the butler, who informed her that she should make her way to the library. This she did, only to find that she was the only person there. She walked to the window and stared for some time at that part of the garden where the recent terrible drama had taken place.

She heard the door open and looked around to see Wenzel Balthasar enter the room. He was tall but somewhat portly and walked with a slow, deliberate air. Although they had been briefly introduced during her first week, he was seldom to be seen, often absent in London and, when in Grove Hall, fond of taking to the fields with his hunting rifle.

"Miss Smy, it is indeed a great pleasure to see you again."

"*Und es ist mir eine große Freude, Sie wiederzusehen, Herr Balthasar.*"

"Miss Smy, you impress me! Can I tell you something? You are the first person to have greeted me in my own language since I have been in England. The British are indeed great, but they might do better to realise that the world is populated by those that prefer to hold conversations in their own language."

"Life has been good to me. It has thrown certain people in my way who've been generous with their time. Tell me, is the language that Austrians speak the same as those born in Germany?"

"Oh, if I might steal something from your unfortunate Oscar Wilde, we are two cultures separated by a common language. Perhaps it is safer to say that we speak the same language, but a different dialect. Now, please, do take a seat."

Smy sat down and realised that this was the third time that she had occupied the same divan, having conversed with both Mrs Balthasar and Inspector Tranmer from the same position in the room.

"Miss Smy, could I ask your opinion on something? I fear we are living in troubled times. Britain, Russia and France seem to have become the most unlikely bedfellows, do you not think? And I am worried that Germany might feel as if they are being encircled by a malevolent alliance. What is your view?"

"You place me at a disadvantage, Herr Balthasar. I..."

At this moment, Mrs Balthasar entered the room, at which point Herr Wenzel Balthasar immediately rose to acknowledge her. Miss Smy also stood up, glad that the interruption had been so fortuitous.

"Wenzel, are you being beastly to our Miss Smy? Miss Smy, I apologise but my husband is exceedingly tiresome when it comes to politics. He would waylay the humblest gardener to ask their opinion on the consequences of the Russo-Japanese war. Wenzel, you are quite impossible. Now do sit down, Miss Smy, so that I might turn our minds to more pressing matters."

Smy sat down first and watched as Mr and Mrs Balthasar also

sat on the opposite couch.

"May I ask how Melka is? I have not seen her recently."

It was Mrs Balthasar who replied. "She is in low spirits, as you would expect. The funeral of her father was traumatic for both her and her mother. I told her that you were here this afternoon, but I could not persuade her to come down to greet you. I am sure you will understand why."

"She is here then and not with her mother?"

The two Balthasars looked uncomfortable with the question, and it was Herr Balthasar who rose and inquired, "Perhaps we might all like some tea?"

"Why, yes, Wenzel. That would be an excellent idea."

"Perhaps I might see Melka? I am aware that..."

"No. I do not think that would help." Mrs Balthasar looked around to make sure that her husband had left the room. "Miss Smy, this is extremely awkward for me, but I have taken the decision to let you go."

"Let me go? Are you saying..?"

"I think that you are a very excellent teacher and, in time, it would be propitious to re-engage you. But we are, as I am sure you will understand, going through a very traumatic time. Melka is in the most regrettable state of mind and I am certain you would find her quite unreceptive to your talents. I will pay you to the end of the month, of course, but must insist that you have no contact with my...my goddaughter again until I give you leave to do so."

Winifred Smy felt quite unable to make rational sense of exactly what was being said and therefore employed the me-chanical techniques that she had learned to adopt whenever she had utterly failed to comprehend the illogical processes of other people. She said nothing; she rose from her chair and made sure that she had everything that she had entered the room with.

"Then I will not trouble you any longer, Mrs Balthasar. I am sorry that, despite all that has happened, you will not permit me to continue seeing Melka, but I fully respect your decision."

As she walked from the room, Cavenham was waiting in the hall as if he'd been expecting her early departure. She caught in his humourless face the smug expression of one whose mean opinion of her had been vindicated.

Calmly, she walked from the front of the house to where she had left her bicycle. There stood Augustus, holding a knife provocatively up in front of his face. She looked down to see that the rear tyre of her bicycle had been sliced open.

10

A GOOD COMPANION SHORTENS
THE LONGEST ROAD

As Miss Smy drew level with Pip's Peace, still pushing her bicycle with its now shredded tyre, she became aware that a cyclist was gaining on her from behind.

"Inspector Tranmer. Were you going my way?"

Tranmer braked and dismounted expertly from his still-moving bike.

"Indeed. Can we start again? I must confess I found our last meeting in Grove Hall a little unpleasant."

"I'll put it down to the anxiety a policeman naturally is subject to when investigating a murder case."

"Please, Miss Smy, it is not a murder case. In fact, I have good evidence to now support my original view that it was a self-inflicted accident. You know far better than I do that when someone goes hunting and carries a gun, these things are very likely to happen. Here, you've got a flat tyre. When did that happen?"

"Your powers of observation have not diminished, Inspector. One can quite appreciate why the East Suffolk Constabulary were so delighted to recruit their Yorkshire miracle."

"I'll ignore that. Here, let me push your bike and you can push mine. It would be easier for you."

"No, thank you. I am quite able to take care of my own bicycle. You said you have 'good evidence'. What good evidence might that be?"

"That it was a very unfortunate accident and not the penny dreadful murder you were so cocksure of."

"Well, Grove Hall has all the gothic grandeur that would give the perfect backdrop to any penny dreadful. But I am convinced Mr Eary's death was murder and therefore fascinated to know what your evidence might be to convince me that it wasn't."

"Fact: Mr Eary was in the woods at the bottom of Grove Hall's estate. Fact: he was carrying a shotgun because he was hunting hares. The wood is well known for them. Whilst creeping surreptitiously through the undergrowth, he sees his daughter Melka and her governess out on the lawn. As he crept nearer the edge of the wood, he inadvertently stumbled and the gun discharged into his chest. He instantly fell out of the bushes onto the lawn, staggered for a few steps and collapsed. I would surmise that by the time that Melka and yourself had reached him, he was already dead."

"I agree with you first and last, Inspector."

Tranmer stopped walking, so surprised was he by Miss Smy's apparent acceptance of his explanation.

"You do?"

"Oh, yes. First and last. Your first statement and your last statement were correct. All that was between, however, was utter poppycock. Of the two 'facts' that you so pompously heralded as evidence, one was a fact, the other a groundless supposition. Now let's get on to Kenton. I have some vegetables to prepare."

So used to Winifred Smy's lofty behaviour was Tranmer, that such a withering critique of his opinions raised only a knowing smile.

"Of course," he countered, catching up with her once more. "I am only a policeman so would have little knowledge of such things."

"Leaving aside your sarcasm, you are prey to something quite peculiar to so many men. You state something as a fact and then, in your mind, it becomes so. You remind me of Manners' dictum that first one finds the story and then pursues the facts that will support it. I can see just why the constabulary and journalism have forged such a convivial relationship."

"Ah, that reminds me. Mr Manners asked me to pass something on to you. He had intended to write but when I told him that I was on my way to Grove Hall this morning, asked if I might tell you personally."

"You see? Proof of the unhealthily close kinship I was just talking about."

"Oh well, if you'd rather not know..." Tranmer teasingly replied.

"Don't play puerile games with me, Inspector."

"Herbert."

"I have rather a short fuse this afternoon and would appreciate it if you would either relate Mr Manners' message or keep it to yourself. But, please, do not play these tiresome games with me."

Tranmer shot a sidelong glance at his fractious walking partner.

"He told me to tell you that Mrs Balthasar was not the godmother of Melka Eary. She wasn't even present at the child's baptism. He also said he has found another connection that you will be very interested in, but he needs to get a clear confirmation of it first."

Winifred Smy remained silent, impassively staring ahead as she walked. Eventually, she replied with only one word, "Perplexing."

The day was turning humid and the air sagged with the weight of the heat. Over their heads, the sky was veiled by a smudge of whitish cloud that seemed to be imperceptibly lowering itself over the landscape, like a heavy bed sheet descending onto a mattress. A group of poppies, more pink than the usual blood red, had opened their frail petals to the ravenous bees that darted and dipped in and around their bruised cavities.

"And nothing else from Mister Manners? Just what you have told me?"

"That was all he asked me to relay to you."

"Then we must wait for Mr Manners to make a connection. I wonder if it is the same one that has occurred to me."

"I beg your pardon?"

"Oh, nothing. Do forgive me, when you live alone you tend to have such silly conversations with yourself."

"I know that, Miss Smy. Living alone is something I also have too much experience of."

"Of course. That was rather unfeeling of me."

As they were nearing the outskirts of Kenton village, Winifred Smy noticed a sudden awkwardness in Tranmer's manner. "Is something troubling you, Inspector?"

"Yes, I'm afraid something is. I...I have always felt rather foolish about my behaviour last summer...at Monk Soham."

"Ah, that."

"Yes, that. I have no excuses. Not even the excuse of too

much good wine. To be very honest with you, I hated myself for my forwardness that evening. You were right to be angry. Anyway, I just wanted to say how sorry I was."

"I was rather sorry myself. Perhaps I am naive in these matters, but I don't believe I gave you any indication that my feelings were other than a respect for your office and a fondness for your company."

Tranmer said nothing but smiled rather vaguely to show that he was trying to understand her point of view.

"You see," Winfred Smy continued. "I have arrived at an opinion about relationships. To a certain extent, when two people first meet - depending on the two who are taken with each other - there is the most fierce heat. But that heat subsides and is then replaced by a comfort and familiarity with each other's company, But, alas, that comfort eventually turns to resentment. The resentment that, were one not drawn into the frenzy of the first attraction, one's life would have taken a very different course. I never want to feel that resentment, Herbert. And that's why I feel that the small distance that separates us is such an ideal one."

Tranmer was hurt by the fact that his affection had been so obviously proscribed by Smy's opinion of him. He searched for something that might explain his emotions, but the true words - the right words - fiendishly eluded him and he thought it best to change the subject.

"I was at Grove Hall myself this morning. Tell me, do I detect a certain frostiness in the servants' attitude to you? I thought they were rather reluctant to bring you into their evidence when I interviewed them."

"Then you do not understand the curious position a governess holds within any household. She is looked down on by the family that employs her, and distrusted by the servants that surround her. Within the house, she is neither fish nor fowl. Many years ago, when I was the governess for Lord Kenilworth, I always dined alone. Governesses are not welcome above or below stairs which is why so many grow forbidding and distant in their later – and very lonely – years. Perhaps, as I was just trying to explain, that might explain a little of why I seek friendships without commitment to anything other than just the comfort of companionship."

"There are depths to you I will never fathom, Miss Smy. I only ever feel I am close to you when we play music together."

"Then let us be close again. Have you something we can study together?"

"Well, funnily enough, I have just picked up a minuet by Beethoven. The story goes that he had originally arranged it for a full orchestra but only the piano accompaniment has survived. Which is very fortunate as I know an extremely excellent pianist who lives rather near to where we are right now."

"Well, whoever that extremely excellent pianist is whom you had in mind, I must disappoint them and insist that you play your minuet only with me, Herbert. Are we agreed?"

"Most certainly. I will inform her immediately that the position of accompanying pianist is already taken."

Miss Smy thought about how much she enjoyed Tranmer's company and, after the vicissitudes of the morning, how glad she was that he had caught up with her. She had thought, when she'd set out on her journey, that the awkward scraping of the ruined bicycle tyre was an auditory leitmotif that had represented her sullen mood. But Tranmer's presence on the walk had made her forget that it was even there.

It was Tranmer who broke the silence. "What do you make

of them at Grove Hall?"

"The Balthasars?"

"All of them. I'd be interested to know."

Winifred Smy thought carefully, taking so long to reply that Tranmer had thought she might have forgotten that he had even asked her.

"The kitchen staff and the gardeners are all local people and seem sensible enough. Melka is confused and grieving. Confused as to why her parents released her into the care of the Balthasars in the first place and, as for her grief, I don't need to explain that."

"No, indeed," interrupted the Inspector. "I can only hope that she has the resilience in time to recover."

"Oh, she'll never recover. She may spend her adult years outwardly coping with life but the spectre of these days will always be a dark shadow that slouches in the corner of her mind."

Tranmer slowly nodded his head. "And the others?"

"I believe Mr Balthasar to be a decent man, but there is something amiss about the others. For example, Mrs Balthasar. Why would she lie about being at a baptism, and even try to convince me that she was not only present but that she was also the godmother? And why return to this part of Suffolk in particular? Occasionally I detect a hint of a Suffolk accent that she tries to hide beneath her formal manner, but she is distant and goes to great pains to limit conversation whenever she can."

"Perhaps Grove Hall was the only suitable property available?"

Winifred Smy's face registered disagreement with Tranmer's suggestion. "No, for whatever reason, I don't think that is the case."

"What do you make of her stepson? I find him patronising and pretentious. In God's name, he's only sixteen now. Just how insufferable will he be when he's older?"

"Oh, we are one on that matter, Inspector. He and his father are poles apart. Herr Balthasar is a man who behaves with a strict sense of decorum. His son has nothing of the manners and kindliness of his father."

"And Berthe? Apparently, she has worked for Mrs Balthasar for some years. Quite devoted to her, I'd say."

"A singular woman. There are strange depths to her, depths that one might do well to leave unstirred. No, I have misgivings there in the same way that I have my doubts about the butler, Cavenham. Everything about him seems so mechanical; he carries out his duties with great care, yet little thought. He seems to be an empty husk of a man, quite devoid of any inner life. But these are just my rather shallow thoughts."

"If your thoughts are shallow, God knows what that makes my thoughts. I have to say that I agree on all fronts. Oh, by the way, a rather intriguing detail emerged from my conversation with the doctor who examined Eary's body. There appeared to be a great deal of bruising on one side of his neck. That was a bit of a surprise."

"Really, Herbert? Now that doesn't surprise me at all. I noticed it immediately when I reached Mr Eary's body."

"You never said."

"Oh no, Inspector: you never asked."

11

SUCH A DANCEN MAN

"Who did you say it was?"

"A Miss Smy, Melka's governess."

A silence followed as the person who had asked the question, hidden from view in an unseen area of the cottage, was now mulling over her decision.

"Let her come in."

Winifred Smy followed the person who had first greeted her; she led her along the cross passage of the cottage and into a small room where a modest fire was burning. To one side of the fire sat a woman of middle age, her hair pulled severely back and held in place by a tortoiseshell comb. She wore the simple clothes of a farmer's hand's wife, and held a grey shawl about her, pulling it close with both hands. The woman who had shown Winifred Smy into the room sat down on a small chair by the window.

"I know what you're thinken. You're thinken why's she got that fire burnen in the middle of summer. I'll tell yew why, my lady. It's 'cos I can't stop feelen the cold. My Tommy's death 'as laid me so very low and very cold. Dew sit yew down there."

"I'll make a pot o' tea, Ella. Miss Smy, would yew like a cup?"

"I would. That would be very welcome."

The woman put down the knitting that she had only just recommenced, and went out to the kitchen.

"Governess, eh? How is Melka?"

"Quite devastated. When did you last see her?"

Mrs Eary didn't respond but fixed her gaze on the small leaps of flame in the grate. Smy continued to watch her. Through the single window that lit the room, a thrush was arrogantly throwing out into the immediate neighbourhood the most beautiful song, confident that it could replicate such beauty at any moment. The spit and crackle of the fire reminded Winifred Smy that the room was unbearably hot and she loosened a button of her blouse.

"We were dancen, you know. A fiddler was playen such a fierce tune, an' he put his strong arm about my waist and pulled me into the dance. Such an 'andsome chap. Big brown pools 'is eyes were. Eyes you could swim in. 'Don't yew 'ave ideas about Tommy Eary', my friend says. 'There's not a girl that dussent 'ave 'im in their sights,' they said. But I pretended I wasn't interested in Tommy Eary. An' that did the trick. That did the trick roight enough."

"How old were you?"

"Sixteen, mebbe seventeen. I never did larn to read an' that. But he made me so happy, the big 'ol fool did. Such a dancen man. As light as a feather, he wuz. There isn't a man in Suffolk who could dance like my Tommy."

"Mrs Eary, what do you think happened at Grove Hall? Why was Tommy there?"

Ella Eary slowly shook her head, her lips tightly compressed to hold back the tears that, once more, wanted to streak down her face. "I carn't for the life of me think why he was there. 'E just said 'e was off to the market to look at some pans 'e knew they were sellen. That 'e might be a little late what with him 'aving a drink with his cronies at the inn. Before 'e went, 'e came up behind me when I was at the tub pouren over the boilin' water and gave me such a squeeze. I told 'im to stop being' so for'ard and to get gooen. An 'e laughed his laugh, kissed my neck and went away. So 'appy 'e were. An' now...an' now..."

Miss Smy went over and placed an arm around Ella Eary, as the sobs convulsed her body. Outside in the warm air, the thrush continued its song with a cold disregard for the troubles of its human neighbours.

Presently, tea was brought in and all three women resumed their original positions as if they'd been actors in a child's toy theatre.

"Dew yew drink that, Ella. Come on now."

"You are a godsend, Mrs Everson. A godsend and no mistake."

Miss Smy recognised the name immediately and looked at Mrs Everson with a particular interest. She was about to ask her if she was indeed Melka's godmother but, having decided that Manners had probably been around and about very recently, thought better of it. Instead, she returned to Ella Eary and inquired, "Had things been very difficult lately for you and Mr Eary?"

"That's a peculiar question. Whatever made you think of it?"

"Well, to have been found poaching..."

Ella Eary immediately stood up, her shawl slipping backwards onto the chair. "How dare you! Poachen? My Tommy? 'E was never a perfect man, but 'e was never a poacher.'

Winifred Smy decided to push the subject. "But I was told he shot himself with his own gun..."

"A lie. A lie, I tell you. There was never a more careful man with a gun in this parish. Ask anyone. Ask anyone yew please. 'E was as careful as careful could be. An' I'll tell you another thing while I'm at it, 'e never poached in 'is entire life. An 'e would certainly never poach from the land of Mrs Balthasar. You're as dawzled as that stupid man who called here yesterday. You all ask the same questions. You all jump to the wrong conclusions. Poachen? My Tommy? I've never 'eard such a load of ol' squit."

Winifred Smy retained her usual icy demeanour while Ella Eary upbraided her for her suggestion. As always, whenever she was the recipient of a verbal volley that was violently conveyed, she remained perfectly calm, almost as if she had - at that very moment - been listening to a recital of her favourite poem. When Ella Eary had decided to sit down in her chair once more, Miss Smy moved to the edge of her seat.

"Can I tell you something? Although I fear what I have to say might be very distressing for you."

"I am already too upset for words. What can you possibly tell me that would upset me again?"

The heat in the room was now intolerable. Winifred Smy glanced quickly at Mrs Everson before looking once more at a troubled Mrs Eary.

"Mr Eary's accident...it wasn't an accident."

Ella Eary did not reply. The calmness of her features made Winifred Smy realise that what she had to say was not an original thought to Ella Eary.

"Mrs Eary, I think..."

"Yew think my Tommy was murdered, don't yew?"

Miss Smy looked once more at Mrs Everson, who was now

engrossed in her knitting and seemed to think of herself as *persona non grata* in the conversation.

"I'm afraid I do. There is something not right about his death. I don't know for certain what it is, but I can't rest until I find out what really happened."

"I would like to help you, Miss Smy. Believe me, I really would. But I don't think I can."

Ella Eary's words took Miss Smy aback for some moments but then she eased into her chair and relaxed. Sipping her tea, she watched Mrs Eary's anxious fingers push her teacup around in its saucer. The thrush's song had stopped. Perhaps it had taken up a new position in its territory.

After some minutes, Winifred Smy rose and thanked Mrs Everson for the tea. She then turned to Ella Eary and said, "Of course, you can't help me. I know that if you were to help me, then that would mean you going back on a promise you once gave someone. I think the same applies to you, Mrs Everson."

As she was about to leave, Smy suddenly turned once again to Mrs Eary and asked, "I know this sounds like a very bizarre request, but would you mind if I looked at your ears?"

12

A TESTING TIME FOR GASPARD

It wasn't until Winifred Smy had drawn level with the imposing oak tree that stood proud above a hedge of hawthorn that she became aware of someone sitting with their back against it.

"Ah, it is Miss Smy! How enchanting."

"I fear you are merely playing the sophisticated Frenchman abroad, Monsieur Gaspard. You probably think that all English women are feeble-minded and quite unable to resist your Gallic charm."

Gaspard stood up and brushed the seat of his trousers. "Mademoiselle Smy, you are quite incorrigible. I am indeed enchanted to make your acquaintance once more. Now, tell me, where are you heading for?"

"Only Debenham. I have one or two things to deal with."

Gaspard meticulously picked each goosegrass seed from his jacket before beaming at Miss Smy. "Debenham? Why that was exactly where I was going. What an astonishing coincidence."

Winifred Smy walked ahead whilst Gaspard continued to attend to his dress. With a few swift steps, he caught up and adjusted his pace to hers. "Such a beautiful day, Miss Smy. No?"

"Indeed. You don't have your usual walking stick with you. Have you brought the wrong one?"

"Oh...oh, this." Gaspard looked at the walking stick with a sense of mild disgust. "No, I have lost my walking stick. I can't think where. Colonel Capon insisted I use one of his, but...well, I don't want to appear ungrateful by refusing the Colonel's kind offer."

"Somehow, you don't strike me as the sort of person who would leave home without your preferred walking stick."

"And you don't strike me as the sort of person who would have any interest in a gentleman's walking stick. Perhaps there is more behind your question, Mademoiselle?"

"It was just an observation. Isn't this avenue of limes quite glorious? The smell of lime trees is utterly intoxicating but I fear you might be just too late in the year now to appreciate that."

Gaspard turned and enthusiastically replied, "Oh yes, I'm sure it must be intoxicating indeed. Colonel Capon told me that he loves the sound of the bees when he walks along here. He said that when he looks up, each tree is alive with them."

Smy looked across at the wide Suffolk landscape that lazily draped itself beneath the sky. Various birds flew across their path in a blur of motion, and nervous rabbits appeared some distance ahead of them, ready to leap back into the hedge as both approached.

"Tell me, Monsieur Gaspard, are you a dilettante who has more money than he knows what to do with, or have you some employment?"

Gaspard laughed at the question. "Oh, I would love to be a

man of leisure, but I work like so many others."

"So what is your occupation? I had you down as somewhat of a drifter. You know, a little work here, a little work there."

Gaspard laughed again. "That would be nice, but I am forced to work against my will."

"Who forces you to do so?"

"I do, I'm afraid. Working for myself was the worst career decision I have ever taken. Despite my outward appearance to appear to all as a reasonable, modern man, I am a very difficult person to work for, Miss Smy."

"And what is your profession?"

"My profession? Why, it is music! Oh yes, I am the music critic for *Le Petit Parisien.* It is a most excellent *journal* and very popular."

"Yes, I know it well. But how wonderful that you are a music critic. I adore music and try to keep up with all that is happening around the world. Tell me, what was the first night of Prokofiev's *'The Rite of Spring'* really like? Here in England, we hear such confusing stories. That it had been badly received by the audience. That Diaghilev himself had to quickly run backstage to help the dancers keep in time with the music. Are these things true or just flights of some journalist's fancy?"

"Oh, it was a most unusual night. Unfortunately, I couldn't be there, I was trying to deal with other matters."

"Other matters? Surely the music critic of one of the most prominent Parisian papers would have been at such a performance as a matter of course? The *Ballet Russes?* Nijinsky? Prokoviev? Diaghilev? One of the most important musical events of the century and you're telling me you were dealing with other matters?"

Gaspard held his walking stick across the path of Winifred

Smy and looked searchingly at her whilst he spoke. "Miss Smy, when we last met, I shared my admiration for your gifts. Colonel Capon himself has related to me the unhappy mysteries that you have been so adept at solving. But, for all how I may appear to you, I am not some convenient character in the drama of your imagination. Your awkward tests of my profession - twice I think you mentioned it - were somewhat insulting. You know as well as I do that it was Igor Stravinsky who composed *'The Rite of Spring'*, and not his compatriot, Sergei Prokofiev. Let us drop this pretence of our casual conversation somehow becoming a search for clues to serve your amateurish intentions."

Gaspard slowly lowered his stick whilst his face lit up with an enthusiastic bonhomie. "Now, I have talked too much! Show me the way to Debenham!"

Winifred Smy did not reply at first, and it was sometime after they had left the lime-lined avenue before she responded. "You are quite right, Monsieur Gaspard. I must confess to having my doubts about you. But I feel that this conversation has clarified so much for me, and I thank you for that."

"We can let the matter rest there, I think. Now, how long to Debenham?"

"Twenty minutes or so. This heat is quite oppressive, isn't it?"

"Are you sure you're not married, Miss Smy?"

"You know I'm not. We clarified that matter when we first met. Why do you ask?"

"Because I find it impossible to understand why a woman like you would not be married. Forgive my impertinent question, but has anyone ever asked you?"

Winifred Smy held back for some moments. It gave her the space to think through her answer. "I would rather not say."

Gaspard comically echoed her reply. "Rather not say? Is there something you are hiding?"

"Yes, Monsieur Gaspard. There is something I am hiding in the same way that you and I both know that there is something you are hiding. You are extremely welcome here in Suffolk. But I know that you are not here out of some desire to travel this county - or to visit Colonel Capon for that matter. You are here for some other purpose and, as much as you will try to conceal it, that purpose will reveal itself in good time."

Gaspard laughed heartily. "Wonderful. Wonderful, Miss Smy! You infuse my dull life with so much meaning. If only it were true. Ah no, dear woman. I am just a simple Frenchman who has found himself strangely mixed up in the most intriguing circumstances. I did not think, for one moment, that my visit would stimulate such interest."

"I take it that when you say 'intriguing circumstances', you are referring to the death of Mr Eary?"

"Of course. You British love your little mysteries. Tell me, Miss Smy, how do you find the Balthasars?"

"The Balthasars? You ask as if you already know them. Do you?"

"Pah! Of course not! It was just a question! You read too much into my poor English, Mademoiselle. Things often get lost - or misinterpreted - in translation."

Gaspard could see that Smy was unconvinced by his explanation. She turned and looked ahead at the field path that would take them towards Debenham. "I'm sure you're right. Come now, Monsieur Gaspard, you go first. Your stride is so much quicker than mine."

13

MEETING A BUNNY FOR TEA

The train from Haughley had been late arriving. As the train, now approaching the station at Ipswich, began to slow down, Winifred Smy took out the letter she had received from Nigel Manners only the previous morning.

My dearest Miss Smy

True to my word I have persevered with discovering what I could related to the curious enigma that is Mrs Balthasar. I took the trouble of visiting Grove Hall under the guise of asking if she would like to take out a notice in our newspaper expressing her condolences for Mr Eary, especially as there was a supposed connection between herself and the deceased. She was reluctant to do so but I persisted in our conversation and noticed that she said to her butler, and I quote, "Cavenham, tell Mr Balthasar that I will be in for lunch shortly, for I am now with a newspaper gentleman."

I have lived in Suffolk too long not to recognise that she used the Suffolk dialect word 'now' instead of the more usual 'just'. So, I asked her if she hailed from these parts and she eventually admitted that she was born in France but had spent a large part of her childhood in Suffolk. Her father was English and, some years before she was born, had left Suffolk to work in France at the invitation of the Duc D'Aumale.

I'm afraid that, at this point, I suspected that she was feeling that she may have been too candid with me, and the most frosty manner was immediately evident. I made my apologies for taking up so much of her time and left.

I have, as I hope Inspector Tranmer related to you, chanced upon something I am still waiting for verification on from a colleague who works in Paris. If the missive bears the news that I am hoping for, then I will relay it to you as soon as I can. But in the meantime, I thought it most expedient for you to meet another contact whom I believe will have information that you might find of interest.

Since I have learned that you are now at leisure once more due to the ending of your employment with the Balthasars, I have taken the liberty of arranging for you to meet my contact so that you may question him yourself. His name is Bunny Bridges and I have asked him to meet you at the Station Hotel in Ipswich at 11.30 am. I do hope you don't think me too forward in arranging this without seeking your agreement first.

I continue to remain your most affectionate and humble servant, Nigel Manners, esq.

P.S. I am engaged to be wed! I know that this will be somewhat of a disappointment to you as I feel that you and I have an understanding that inevitably leads to the greatest commitment one can undertake to another. But I am sure that you will soon come to terms with my withdrawal from the 'most marriageable young men' list (My little joke! I know that no such list exists) and will find, in time, a husband to call your own.

The very idea of Manners having referred to himself as a 'humble servant' brought a smile to Miss Smy, who gathered her things ready to alight from the train. The Station Hotel, located just outside the station itself, was reached in a very short time. Standing outside was a rather dapper man, small in stature but sporting the most impressive moustache that curled away from his nostrils with something of a triumphal display. His eyes, though small, seemed to be lit with an unmistakable happiness as if he had known nothing but joy and contentment his entire life.

"Mr Bridges?"

"Ah, you must be Miss Smy. A pleasure, ma'am. Call me Bunny. Everyone calls me Bunny."

Winifred Smy suggested tea in the hotel restaurant, and it was there that they both settled into their seats. The tablecloths were smoothed with not a crease to be found. Bunny eyed it with some wonder. "Why, dew yew look at that. Fit for an altar, that is."

"Bunny, Mr Manners told me that you used to work with horses. I take it that would have been on Nacton Heath. It used to be quite popular."

"Oh, pop'lar when I started as a lad. They did both flat racing and jumps in those days, but people now have lost interest. Closed it three year ago. Sad to see but there yew go."

"I don't know if Mr Manners told you, but I'm trying to trace a family who worked there. I understand there was a rumour that they left England to work in France. Is this true, Bunny?"

"'Tis true enough. But it weren't no family. If it's the man yer thinken of, then it's likely to be Arthur Goymer. He'd no family but 'is frail ol' mum, when he wuz at Nacton. There wasn't a finer man with 'orses than Arthur Goymer. Thas why the word got round and some French lah-di-dah offered him a job. Now, dew yew pass that sugar bowl, please."

Winifred Smy watched as he placed two cubes of sugar onto

his napkin. "So this Arthur Goymer was single when he went to France?"

Bunny Bridges looked up and smiled. "Single when he left Ipsidge. But not fer long. Any sign of that tea yet?"

Smy looked around but the serving staff were still occupied with other guests. She looked at Bunny Bridges and felt a warmth about him: his clear green eyes, the openness of his face and the uncomplicated manner of his personality.

"Where did he go to, our Mr Goymer?"

"Oh, Chantilly. He worked for the rich and famous so 'e did. The course in them days wuz owned by the Duc D'Aumale. Goymer said that this duke looked him out personally. And then Goymer married a French lady, so we heard." Bunny Bridges grinned as thoughts from long ago returned and ran before him. "Such a clever man. Meant for better things than what we 'ad to offer, Miss Smy. Course, we never saw 'im again. Why would 'e come back? His life was a long way from old Nacton Heath."

"Did he and his new French wife have any children at all?"

"Family?" Bridges was unprepared for the question and sat back, screwing his face up in thought. "Family? Why, I don't... no, hang on, there was a young one that I 'ears of. Little girl. Yes, someone told me that Goymer's mother used to speak about her little French granddaughter."

"So Arthur Goymer left the racecourse at Nacton Heath after being employed by this Duc D'Aulame and moved to France to be part of his horse racing retinue at Chantilly? And, if I understood you correctly, whilst he was there he met a French woman and they had a daughter?"

"Tea?" asked the waitress. She placed the crockery and teapot onto the ice-white tablecloth with an odd mixture of decorum and boredom.

"Thank you," said Miss Smy, who pushed a cup and saucer close to Bunny Bridges. He, in turn, offered to Miss Smy to draw the first cup from the pot.

"No, I prefer my tea very strong, so you go first, Bunny."

"Me too," Bunny replied, sitting back in his chair.

"Did Goymer's mother ever meet her granddaughter?"

"Well, yes, funnily enough. 'Cos they sent their daughter to Suffolk. Then, when ol' Mrs Goymer died, it wuz the Earys that looked after 'er. And then she went back to France."

Miss Smy poured tea into the two cups and tried hard to not reveal any emotion to what Bunny was saying. "Why do you think they sent the daughter to England, Bunny? That seems a strange thing to me."

"Oh, because old Goymer per'aps 'ad it in his 'ead that she must go to Ipsidge School, I don't know why. Not that he'd been there himself, of course. Mebbe 'e 'ad the idea that that was what real eddication was."

"And what was the daughter's name?"

"Now you are asking. Something like Vera... Verona... Veronica...yes, I think thas it, it wuz Veronica."

"Veronica. Or Véronique, as the French would prefer to say it."

"I dussent know about any Véronique. Just plain Veronica wuz what I wuz told. Mind if I give the pot a stir?"

"Stir away."

Bunny Bridges removed the lid and agitated the brewing tea with a spoon before pouring it out into the two cups. "Hoity-toity, she wuz. Only a little mawther, but hoity-toity nonetheless. Thas what I heard, Miss Smy. Milk?"

"Please. How old was she when she arrived in Suffolk?"

Bunny rested the teapot on the table and, once more, screwed up his face in thought. "Four, mebbe five years old. The older I get, the harder I find it to pin down someone's age."

Smy laughed. "Me too, Bunny. And when Véronique left Suffolk? How old then?"

Bunny Bridges now opened his napkin and dropped the two sugar cubes into his tea with the reverence of a priest observing the sacrament of holy communion. "Almost grown up, I'd say. I mean, I wouldn't know for certain, but she was about sixteen, even a bit older."

"And Arthur Goymer, her father. Did you ever see him again?"

"No. We lost Arthur to the French and 'e never came back to Nacton. Why would 'e? Tommy and 'is wife never saw the girl, this Veronica, again when she went back ter France. That wuz such a terrible thing to 'appen to old Tommy Eary, Miss Smy. He doted on that girl, so I understand. And now poor Tommy's dead, god rest 'is soul."

"Yes, I was there."

"When he wuz shot?"

"Well, they say it was self-inflicted. An accident."

Bridges became uneasy and writhed a little in his chair. "Wasn't an accident. Tommy Eary? There's something not right in all of this. I 'eard about what 'ad happened and it just dussent make sense."

"Why not, Bunny?"

"He was allus too particular. And I never knew a better, more careful man to carry 'is gun, ever. Accident? Thas a rum 'un."

They finished their tea in silence. Both knew what the other was thinking. Why was Eary in the wood that day? And who would want him dead?

Miss Smy summoned the surly waitress and paid the bill

without leaving her a tip. She grudgingly thanked Smy for her payment and cleared away the cups and saucers.

"If it wasn't an accident, the way that old Eary died, then who would want to shoot him like that?"

Miss Smy gathered her change and let it slip from the palm of her hand into her purse. "Oh, I think I know who might have killed Mr Eary. I just can't work out why."

14

AN UNEXPECTED RENDEZVOUS

Miss Smy couldn't sleep. She sat up and moved her pillow around to what she hoped was a more comfortable position, but soon found that the thoughts and anxieties that had woken her up were still careening in and out of every pathway in her brain. She flung the covers back and resolved to wash herself and go for a walk. A glance at her mantle clock told her that it was not yet 5.30 am, but she knew that only a walk in the cool morning air could alleviate the mental discomfort she was feeling.

She turned down Church Lane and on into Bellwell Lane, passing the entrance to Moat Farm. Across the fields, long, curled wreaths of mist had settled, creating a landscape that had slumped into its own blankets, just like the ones that Winifred Smy had so recently forsaken. The air was soothing and her path ahead was only visible through a grey gauze that softened the curves and colours of the trees and hedges. A blackbird flew into her path and, having only just registered that it was sharing that part of the lane with another being, quickly altered its path of flight before rising into the welcoming upper limbs of a statuesque elm.

She loosened her hair and felt the air smoothing across her face as she walked. She knew that the choice to take an early morning stroll had been a sound one, but hadn't it always been so, she realised to herself. Whenever her thoughts had threatened to overwhelm her, or when she needed a precious boundary of space to interrogate her feelings, a simple walk had always provided the perfect panacea.

It was just as she drew level with the small group of trees of Bellwell Plantation, that she noticed a shadowy movement ahead. Her first reaction was one of panic, thinking that her mysterious follower and she were finally about to meet. The figure's gait was slow and deliberate, and there appeared to be something hanging from their right hand that she found hard to make out. In time, as both approached each other, her mind was reassured that there was nothing to fear.

"Bit of a dag, this mornen, Miss Smy?"

"Indeed, but it does lovely things to a landscape, don't you think? Been working, Spadger?" Miss Smy's eyes turned to the three dead rabbits he was holding.

"Oh, these. Why I just picked 'em up off the lane back there. Probably somebody dropped 'em. 'P'raps fell out their bag."

"Of course. And you are going to do the charitable thing and make somebody a gift of them?"

"Well, 'ow did yew know that. That was the hooly thing I intended to do. Drop 'em off to ol' Mrs Kemp up there at Bellwell Cottage. Anyway, as we're askin', you're out awful early."

"Couldn't sleep. So I thought I'd wander out for a couple of miles, just to clear my head."

"Roight enough. It dussant do a man any harm to greet the new day when old Phoebus is doin' much the same. I've also been known to walk out in the very late evening myself, as you well know." With this statement, Spadger winked knowingly at Miss Smy, his forefinger delicately tapping the side of his rosy nose.

"Blaarst me, I nearly forgot! That man you'd asked about."

"You know who he is?"

"That I don't know. But I spoke with young Tatters and Sheddy from Pages Farm and they were certain they didn't know 'im either. They were suspicious of 'im well before he appeared at Pages Farm. You know what it's like round 'ere."

Indeed, Miss Smy was well aware of how hard it was in any Suffolk village to pass through a parish without its inhabitants immediately becoming aware of their presence. Suffolk people were always listening. It could be the swift chirrups of a panicked blackbird or the shrill squark of a flustered pheasant. Not only were animals themselves able to alert each other of a threat or unknown interloper, but every farm worker in Suffolk was attuned to the same sounds as well.

"Sheddy said that it were a rabbit shot out from near the pightle that they wuz clearin' that alerted 'im. Next to ol' Waddledickey Lane. E 'ears the man walken, e' said. Said that there wuz summat rum about the footsteps. So, when the man 'ad passed, 'e crept through the chatter bushes and saw 'im on the path. A limp 'e told me. Bad 'un too. Tom said this furrener had imitate to pass 'im without 'im knowen, but 'e knew."

"Then it's the same man. The man I first became aware of. He had a limp when I saw him walking across the field path that day."

"But thas not all, an' I'm not sure whether I should tell you this or not."

Spadger Peck's face darkened and he hurriedly scratched his

chest and looked away.

"I would rather know, Spadger, than not know."

"Well, of course it's probably nothen, but I did 'ear he wuz in Abbotts, in Deb'n'am. And the ol' mawther there, well, she told me he spoke a bit like an Essex man. And then she told me..."

"She told you what, Spadger?"

"Like I say, it's probably nothen, but 'e bought himself..."

Spadger looked up only to find that Miss Smy's eyes were fully turned on him. He sighed and awkwardly shrugged his shoulders before lifting the peak of his hat.

"A knife, Miss Smy. 'E'd gone and bought hisself a knife."

Winifred Smy's head reeled when she heard the word 'knife'. Her first thought was to remain rational. Wasn't she thinking about this too much? Surely the fact that some stranger in the parish had bought a knife was nothing to do with her? After all, she didn't know for certain that this man was following her. Wasn't it all conjecture on her part? And yet her instincts told her that this person – whoever he was – was somehow here because of her. Had she offended people in the past? Of course she had. She knew that her manner had brought her more than her fair share of enemies. But for any hurtful remark to have come to this? To have upset someone so deeply that she now found herself being stalked on the very roads and field paths that had previously been such a haven for her.

Spadger leaned towards Miss Smy, enquiring. "Yew all right, Miss?"

Miss Smy rallied, "Well, of course, Spadger. Why wouldn't I be? I think I'd best be going home. I'll walk with you up to Mrs Kemp's cottage."

"Thassa gel. Like I said, it's nothen to worry about. Why, I bet 'e's already gorn by now. Yew know how it is. There are a lot of good men moven 'atwin villages, looken for work."

"You're right. But thank you for asking around. It was very good of you to help me. Have you had breakfast? I'd be happy to make you something."

"I appreciate the generosity, but once I've dropped these rabbits on Kemp's doorstep, I'll be headen home. I've an appointment with some pork cheese I've been a saven."

With Spadger's ringing valediction of "Dew yew keep a troshin'" in her ears, Winifred Smy walked back up the lane. Try as she might, the salve that the morning's walk had provided was now firmly dispelled, and her mind once again ricocheted from one troubling thought to another. Ahead, as she rounded the bend before the church, she could see that the sun had lifted itself above the shreds of mist that still clung to the wheat. Reaching her cottage, she closed the gate behind her and opened the door.

Removing her jacket, she caught sight of an envelope on her kitchen table. At first, she was confused because she had no recollection of having left any such letter on her table. She then noticed that it bore no stamp and was neatly addressed with 'To Miss Smy'.

She opened the envelope and pulled out the note which read, *"I want to see you. I will be outside Debenham Church on Tuesday at one o'clock. There is something I need to tell you. Come alone."*

There was no name. Smy's next thought was to see if she recognised the writing, but - as she suspected - it was a confident hand that she couldn't place. The fact that someone had taken advantage of her open front door to leave the letter deeply disturbed her, and she immediately checked every room in her house, fearing that her unwelcome visitor might still be present. Satisfied that she was truly alone, she immediately locked the front and back doors.

It was as she was walking towards the sink, intending to draw water for the kettle, that she stopped. Slowly, she turned to look once more at the table where she had left the now open letter. Her subconscious mind had seen something that her conscious mind now slowly became aware of. Lying across the table was a walking stick. A walking stick that she instantly recognised.

15

AFTER DINNER CONVERSATIONS

"**N**o more wine for me, thank you." As the servant moved away with the bottle, Miss Smy was already regretting what she had just said.

"Are you sure, good lady?" asked the genial host, Colonel Capon.

"Oh, very sure, Colonel. The wine is excellent."

"Indeed so," added the Reverend Pilbeam. "Monsieur Gaspard: a *Saint Julien* appellation?"

But it was Colonel Capon who answered, "This superb *Château Léoville-Las Cases* is indeed the gift of my good friend, Monsieur Gaspard. To have graced me with such an outstanding bottle from one of the greatest years that the region of Bordeaux has ever produced is something I will not forget."

Marc-Antoine Gaspard nodded a gracious acceptance of the Colonel's praise. "I will proclaim to all here assembled, that the 1900 was - *sans aucun doute* - an *annus mirabilis* and I am honoured to share this beautiful wine with such esteemed company."

As he spoke those last words, he looked across the table at

Winifred Smy. She immediately turned to look at Colonel Capon, determined not to allow herself to be unsteadied by Gaspard's searching stare. Was he looking for her reaction or approval? It was difficult to tell.

"Monsieur Gaspard, have you known the Colonel long?" asked Mrs Pilbeam, who was an expert at redirection when she sensed awkwardness in any conversation.

Gaspard delicately dabbed the corners of his mouth with his napkin before fixing his deep blue eyes on Mrs Pilbeam. "My father knew the Colonel many years ago, although the Colonel to this day struggles to remember him."

"Old memory, not what it was! No surprises there!" interjected Colonel Capon.

Gaspard sat up in his seat and laughed at the candour of the Colonel's remarks. "My father would be most aggrieved. He always had such respectful memories of the Colonel."

"So how did they meet?" asked the Reverend Pilbeam.

"He was a military attaché to Great Britain. An expert on the fighting tactics of the local rebel armies in the Far East of which, I am sad to say, there are many. But that is beside the point, my father was always regaling us with the pleasure of his official meetings with the Colonel."

"Couldn't remember the man until Monsieur Gaspard started to talk about his father's time in Hanoi. Ah, I said to myself, I remember that conversation. Good man too, your father. Very good man."

The Reverend Pilbeam held up his finger and announced, "Plants."

"Pardon, Reverend?" asked Gaspard.

"Sorry, Monsieur Gaspard, but did your father bring any plants back? From Vietnam?"

"I regret that, to my knowledge, he did not."

Pilbeam raised his eyebrows in a sorry acceptance and said, rather resignedly, "Well, it was worth asking. I hear that the continent has some quite dazzling flora."

"Oh, Monsieur Gaspard, I quite forgot to mention it, but I have found your walking stick."

Gaspard looked shocked. "My walking stick?"

"Yes, the one that you were carrying when I first met you in All Saints churchyard."

Smy was amazed at the speed of Gaspard's recovery from his initial surprise. "Why, it's wonderful that it has been found. Where did you find it?"

"Where did you lose it?"

"Lose it? I can't recall. One moment I had it with me and then I realised that I must have put it down somewhere. So where had I left it?"

Miss Smy chose not to answer at first. Then she looked momentarily away as if trying to recall where she had alighted upon the lost object. Smiling rather enigmatically, she looked back at Gaspard and casually rejoined with a flippant, "Oh. I forget."

Gaspard didn't reply, but his face fiercely communicated his response that he knew that she was fully aware of where and when she had found his walking stick.

"Then I would welcome the pleasure of visiting your home to collect it. I was most annoyed when I realised it was gone. Your house, Miss Smy, I believe it is the cottage on the other side of the road opposite the church?"

"It is, but you must tell me a time or else I will probably be out. One must make full use of these long days of summer."

"Cigars, Gentlemen!" trumpeted Colonel Capon. All the

diners now rose but in very different ways. The Colonel stood upright with such speed and straightness that his guests would not have been surprised if he had done so to salute the remains of the wine bottle that lay still in its silver casket. Mrs Pilbeam quickly checked in front of her before nimbly leaving her seat whilst her husband pushed backwards with such force that – with slightly more effort – his chair would have been propelled through the tall window immediately behind him. Whereas Smy and Gaspard methodically rose and glanced at each other as if both were gladiators searching for the Achilles heel of their opponent.

The servants slowly began to remove the dishes from the table with the Reverend Pilbeam suddenly lunging back towards where he had been sitting, realising that he had forgotten to take his glass of the remaining precious wine with him.

Winifred Smy, refusing to accept the protocol that she should retire to a neighbouring room to await the conveyance of the men's promise that they would eventually join them in the drawing room, invited Mrs Pilbeam to walk up the lime-lined avenue of Kenton Hall. This was enthusiastically accepted by the vicar's wife and, after exiting the immediate gardens of the hall, they took up a slow and ambling pace.

Towards the west, the sun was lowering itself into a feathering of orange-grey clouds that seemed to be slowly entwining themselves around it. The backdrop of the blue sky was darker overhead but melted to a steely white just above the trees of Aspall woods.

At first, they spoke of local matters: the continuing struggles of the Mid-Suffolk Light Railway; the promise of – with the grace of God – exceptional crop yields this year, and the sinister origin of Olive Cattermole's many bruises.

"And what did you make of Mr Gaspard?" asked Smy, after they had passed Blood Hall cottages.

"Oh, a most handsome man. And those eyes! Quite exceptional. Yes, most winning in his manner and conversation. To a point."

"To a point?"

Mrs Pilbeam stopped and placed her hand on Winfred Smy's arm. "Can I tell you something I have never shared with anybody else? If you are uncomfortable then I will truly understand."

"I don't think – at least I am quite sure – that you would ever make me feel uncomfortable, Mrs Pilbeam."

"You see when I first met my husband, he was the most awkward individual. There, now I feel I'm openly betraying him, telling you this."

"If you would rather..."

Mrs Pilbeam held up her hand and said, "No. I have something I think that's important to say and is germane to your question."

They began to walk on together.

"He truly was embarrassing. So very awkward. In the garden of my mother's house, whilst she was speaking, he suddenly became distracted and left his chair to pursue some moth that had just floated across the lawn. She was appalled! Here was this man, supposedly my putative suitor, deciding that the appearance of some Lepidoptera was more engaging than the conversation of my own mother!"

Smy laughed with Mrs Pilbeam, fully able to imagine the scene she described.

"And so, at that very moment," continued Mrs Pilbeam, "I inwardly and enthusiastically made the decision that this was the very man I should marry. I wanted him first as a most flawed human being, and secondly as a husband. I thank God dearly for that one event on that day in my mother's garden."

They walked on again for some time before Miss Smy broke the silence. "But your original observation - before you spoke about meeting your future husband - was about Gaspard."

"Of course! How silly of me to get distracted like that. As I was saying, my husband is a deeply flawed man. I saw it that day in my mother's garden. But I liked his flaws. This Monsieur Gaspard, though, is the most consummate actor. Altogether a very striking man and so handsome! But there is something of the theatre about him. Now. Here am I wittering on about what I think."

On the lane ahead, a hare emerged from the hedge and, noticing with alarm that it was not alone, skittered along the road with an awkward lope that instantly brought Nigel Manners to Winifred Smy's mind.

Still smiling at the thought of Mr Manners, Smy asked, "Mrs Pilbeam, can I share my thoughts?"

"Why, yes."

"Monsieur Marc-Antoine Gaspard rather frightens me."

"Frightens you? That's odd. He's perfectly amiable to my mind, for all I've just said."

"Oh, but that's the point, isn't it? He's too perfectly amiable."

16

A MINUET'S REST

"Shall we try that again, Herbert?"

"I thought it went rather well. I did fluff the *trio*, I'm afraid. My bowing is not what it should be. How was it for you?"

Miss Smy was looking intensely at her score. "I think the sixths are rather clumsy at the moment in my right hand. It's a very pretty tune though. I do like it. Yes, let's give it another go."

"Yes, very stately. Shall I count us in?"

Miss Smy rested her fingers on the piano keys and glanced at Tranmer to indicate she was ready. Soon, the delicate minuet was dancing across the room, although the players' intense concentration seemed in sharp contrast to the playfulness of the melody. Miss Smy grew angry with herself at one point when she failed to find the very low G in her left hand, but both looked pleased when the short piece was over.

"It's not really a taxing piece, especially for someone of your ability."

Tranmer shook his head, "When you don't practise regularly

enough, then they are all taxing pieces." He wedged his violin back between his neck and collarbone and started to check its tuning. "Could you give me an A, Winifred?"

After both were satisfied that the tuning was once again secure, Miss Smy rose from her piano. She walked over to the large dresser at the end of the kitchen, took out the note that she had received only two days before and gave it to Tranmer. "What do you make of this?"

He sat down, and after taking in the message and studying the paper very closely, rubbed the side of his face in concentration. "Who's it from?"

"My follower."

"Your follower? Do you mean you have an admirer?"

Smy didn't answer but hummed the Beethoven minuet whilst smiling enigmatically. She then thought better of making light of a matter that had given her considerable anxiety and sat opposite Tranmer.

"My follower is, I would hazard, not an admirer. In fact, I have had the unnerving experience of being followed."

"Followed? Are you sure?"

"Herbert, you really can be rather grating sometimes. Of course I'm sure. Not only has this man suddenly appeared at some distance from me on two occasions, he even entered my house whilst I was out and left that note. He also left Monsieur Gaspard's walking stick."

"Who is Monsieur Gaspard? Do I know him?"

"More sherry?"

Tranmer nodded, and Smy continued as she poured his drink. "You probably don't know Monsieur Gaspard. He is staying with Colonel Capon. Apparently, the Colonel knew his father some years ago, although there is something about that connection that I can't quite put my finger on."

"And what's this Gaspard like?"

Smy thought carefully for a moment. "I would say that he is very charming and possesses one gift that would make him extremely attractive to women."

Tranmer narrowed his eyes. "I'm intrigued. What is this special gift?"

"He makes women he talks to feel that all they say is interesting. Whether he genuinely does think it's interesting is another matter. Combine that skill with a very handsome appearance and you have someone that many women would find most desirable."

Tranmer, feeling a little threatened by the exotic presence of Gaspard in the vicinity, quickly changed the subject. "Where did you find the note?"

Smy's eyes directed Tranmer towards the kitchen table.

"And the walking stick? The one that belongs to this Monsieur Gaspard?"

"Also on the table."

"So he let himself into the house? Anything missing when you got back?"

"Not a thing. But it wasn't pleasant knowing that he was in this very room. I will continue to ask around. It is extremely rare for anyone to go unnoticed in Kenton."

Tranmer looked intently at the note once more before leaning across and handing it back to Smy. "And are you going to meet him?"

"Of course. I was very worried for a while. Not least when Spadger Peck recently told me that some man - who no one seems to know - was seen in Abbotts purchasing a knife. But my logical conclusion is that, if he intended to stab me, then he would have already tried to do that."

"What makes you so sure?"

"Oh, because murderers are discreet and most people know that one has a very small amount of time to remain *incognito* in a rural area like ours. Apparently, two brothers who work at Pages Farm - Sheddy and Tatters Farthing - had already seen a strange man on the day I first became aware of him. The second time I saw him was when I was on my way to Grove Hall, and I could clearly see him walking through the middle of a field towards me, which is hardly what one might expect of someone who would want to remain undercover."

"I'm curious as to why he would have this stick as well. You say it belongs to this Gaspard fellow. Where did he find it?"

"Once I have asked this mysterious stranger that very question, I will let you know. Have there been any developments about the murder of Thomas Eary?"

"You aren't going to give this thing up, are you? Don't keep going on about it being a murder when there's no evidence whatsoever to support such a thing. I can't think why you still believe that."

"I knew it was murder from the moment that we turned the body over. That is the fact that I rest my conclusion on. There was also another question that I kept coming back to, and that has now been fully resolved in my mind. If I am right, then that confirms my conviction even more."

"Are you going to tell me what you noticed when you turned the body over?"

Miss Smy stood up from her chair and began to hum the melody of the minuet once again.

"You do know," continued Tranmer, "That it is an offence to withhold information from the police?"

"Oh Herbert, you see I would share it with the police if there was a murder enquiry, but as you have reminded me, it was apparently just an accident. So I must keep my thoughts to myself and not trouble you any more."

Tranmer slapped his legs in exasperation. "I give in. But I have warned you already not to get involved in anything. After all, this is…"

"A man's work? I do hope that wasn't what you were about to say."

Tranmer took up his violin once more and secured it under his chin. "I was about to say 'a police matter', which it very much is."

"I hear your message, loud and clear, Herbert."

"I would rather you *listened* to my message loud and clear, Winifred."

But Smy was already back sitting at her piano and adjusting the sheet music.

"Now, my good Mr Tranmer. Shall I count us in? And do try and keep up with me in the *trio*."

17

THE LONG DRINKING ARM OF THE LAW

It struck Miss Smy that, just like his bicycle, the police uniform belonging to and worn by PC Cornish never quite fitted him. Perhaps the poor man had shrunk slightly since its first fitting, or the uniform was made of a material that was, in time, given to stretching. Either way, George Cornish's body never quite filled out the jacket or trousers of his occupational attire. It was apparent to all that when one witnessed Cornish's inflated view of his importance to the community, he seemed blissfully unaware of his slightly ridiculous appearance. As one local wag put it: Cornish's office did not exist to serve the parish, his parish existed to serve his office.

This being said, the confusing thing was that there was not one person in Debenham - or any of the surrounding parishes - that took against him. Yes, he was pompous. Yes, he was occasionally patronising. But, in his heart, there was a kindly manner that always prevailed. When the occasional crime took place, he never failed to give comfort to the person who had been sinned against. It might be a visit for a cup of tea and some gentle words; it was sometimes a solicitation to the victim's neighbours to 'drop by and see that they are aright'. As the Reverend Pilbeam once opined, "His ego might be all over the place - but his heart is always in the right place."

Looking through the window that morning, Miss Smy pondered these thoughts as PC George Cornish steadied his bike against her fence before knocking at her door. She opened it, smiled warmly at the officer and immediately took down the pewter flagon and half-filled a glass with beer.

"That'll do me no end o' good, Miss Smy. That Bellwell Lane always has the better o' me."

"Put my mind at rest straight away, Constable. Have I done anything wrong? I wasn't expecting a visit from you."

Cornish drew his sleeve across his lips after having imbibed the first long intake of beer. "Wrong? You? Why you'd be the last person I'd be accusin' of any fel...fillon...file..."

"Felony?" suggested Winifred Smy.

"Crime! Crime was what I meant 'er say."

Miss Smy immediately topped up Cornwall's glass, which he pretended to take exception to.

"Now, Miss Smy. Hold yew hard. Yew marn't be fillin' that glass too much as I 'ave work to do."

Miss Smy placed the flagon on the table and played the role of an admonished child. Cornwall immediately reached for his glass and drained the contents in one long draught.

Once more, Miss Smy filled the glass whilst Cornwall explored the various pockets of his uniform. "Now, where was it. Here? No, not here. This one, per'aps? No, not there either..."

With increasing exasperation, PC Cornish explored each of his many pockets several times, his fingers prying, pulling and prodding as they searched out the elusive target.

"Is what you are looking for, for me?"

"Eh? Why yes...I've a note 'ere. Somewhere 'ere. Can't think why...Ah! Found it! Knew I'd brought it."

Eventually, from a pocket which was on the inside of his uniform jacket, he withdrew a folded sheet of paper and, tipping his head slightly backwards to help him focus, he satisfied himself that this was indeed the right piece of paper.

Winifred Smy looked on with affectionate amusement. George Cornish was not only the same age as her father, but they had been close childhood friends. According to her mother, when Daniel Smy had decided to leave behind his farm hand's life and join the army, George Cornish had likewise decided to don a uniform, only he had decided to sign up for the East Suffolk constabulary. Winifred Smy knew that PC Cornish could have just sent the note on to her, but the opportunity to reassure himself that she was well was something he never failed to do.

"Here you are. A note for you."

"Who is it from?"

Cornish screwed his eyes up as he tried to think of the name. "That Grove Hall girl. Eary? Yes, Eary. Why the child's first name..."

"Melka?"

Cornish's lips settled into a large smile, as if glad that his rackety memory would be spared no further discomfort. He reached for his glass and took another satisfying pull on its amber contents.

"It's her chess move, so she told me."

"Chess move?" Smy, a little puzzled, put the note to one side and refilled his glass again. "Can I ask you something,

Constable?"

"T'all depends on what it is!" returned the now slightly bibulous policeman.

"Have you noticed anyone new in the village?"

"Anyone new?" Cornish scratched his neck as he considered her question. "Anyone new...Why, yes. I saw the new farrier from Occold in The Cherry Tree for the first time."

"No one else? Perhaps you might have noticed someone with a limp?"

"A limp? Thas a bit particular. No, can't say I 'ave. Strange question. Why dew yew ask?"

"Oh, because I noticed a man recently whom I'd not seen before. I have also heard from Spadger Peck that Tatters and Sheddy Farthing had also noticed someone strange around Pages Farm."

"Dew yew fill my glass up again and I'll give your question a bit more thought."

Smy stood up and poured the beer into Cornish's glass to the brim. The policeman now took thoughtful sips from the glass and thought deeply about Smy's question. He then drained the rest of the beer, stood up - albeit with a slight wavering - and reached for his helmet.

"No. Can't think of anyone I've seen in Deb'n'ham who's not known to me. Thank you for the 'ospertality, Miss Smy. Allus a good pint from The Crown. I assume that's where it's from?"

"It is indeed."

"May I use the bumby before I go, Miss Smy? I'm sorry to have to ask, but..."

"Not at all! You know where it is in the garden?"

Cornish nodded and left through the kitchen door. Miss Smy took her chance to read Melka's note. In her childish but neat handwriting, she had written:

My dear Miss Smy

I miss you. Nobody will tell me why you left and I am now lonely and very miserable. I miss my Pa. I wake up screaming with nightmares about him. One is where I find his body in the garden and, when he is turned over, his face is ugly and awful. Sometimes I have the same dream and it is not him. I wake up crying every morning and want to leave this awful place.

My godmother is terrible. She keeps telling me to grow up, but she hasn't lost her Pa. Mr Balthasar is very nice but Augustus, his son, is a pig. That's a horrible thing to say about someone, but it's true.

Please Miss Smy, can you not find an excuse to come back to Grove Hall and take me away with you? We can do it in secret if we have to. I could meet you in the woods and you could take me home to Ma. Why doesn't she visit me? I miss her but she has never come to see me. If I don't see someone other than that brute Augustus and my terrible godmother, then I promise I will kill myself. I know it's a sin. But what else can I do? Other than you, Ma and Mr Balthasar, I haven't a friend anywhere in the world.

By the way, I remember you once telling me that you played chess with a friend and you would send notes to each other with your next move on them. I told the policeman that this note was a chess move, pretending we were doing the same thing. You won't tell on me will you? It was the only way I could think of getting a note to you.

Let me know you have got this letter very soon. Can you think of some sign that would let me know? It would help me to cope if I knew you were still my friend.

Affectionately yours

Melka Eary

Miss Smy had just returned the note to a skirt pocket when PC Cornish re-entered the kitchen.

"Can I just ask you when you are returning to Grove Hall?"

"Tomorrer, first thing, as a marra a' fact. Inspector Tranmer wants a poke aroun' in the wood. Can't think why. Perhaps 'e's a bot'nist." Cornish quietly chuckled at his own joke.

Winifred Smy took a small note from her drawer, scribbled something on it and then sealed it quickly into an envelope. "Could you give this directly to Melka? As soon as you get there. Nobody else, you understand. We have been playing chess in secret and this is my next move. She would be in a lot of trouble if anyone found out."

"What did yew say wuz in the note?"

"As I just said, Constable, it's my next move."

$$18$$

A PROMISE FINALLY KEPT

A bright Tuesday afternoon found Winifred Smy pedalling into Debenham to keep the appointment with the stranger who had left her the note. Despite going to bed the night before with certain misgivings of how the meeting would go, she had actually slept well and was now curious as to just what would unfold when they met. Her mind had vacillated that morning between trepidation and inquisitiveness. Who was he and what could he possibly want with her? Of course, she mused, it might all be some terrible hoax and he may even not show up at all.

She had already decided how she would approach the place they were due to meet, which was at St Mary's Church, slightly set back from the road at the top of the hill. She planned to cycle uphill and ride past the church first to allow her the opportunity of reconnoitring the churchyard for the man's presence. Once having passed the church, she intended to turn left after the Woolpack pub before entering the churchyard from the entrance at Cross Green.

Her first pass past the church allowed her the opportunity to scan most of the area surrounding St Mary's; however, no one was to be seen. She then - as she had planned - dismounted at Cross Green and, with her heart beating, walked up the small path that led through the churchyard. She was conscious that there was a small sphere of dread beginning to grow in her mind, and she longed for someone else whom she might know to visit a grave or enter the church for a moment's quiet devotion, just so that she was not alone. Against the wall that ran across the back of the small yard of The Woolpack, rested a large black and white cat, crouched and content, its eyes half-closed in repose.

As she neared the large porch of the church, she saw, seated inside, a man of late middle age with his right leg resting stiffly in front of him. He raised his head when he became aware of Smy and motioned her towards him with his hand. Smy, still unsure of just how close to get, adjusted her hold of the bicycle so that it was between her and the man. She then stopped and, still being some yards away, coolly regarded the stranger. What struck her first - perhaps because she had never been close enough to him before this meeting - was the thickness and length of his beard. Although overwhelmingly grey, there were single streaks of black that ran through it. A wide-brimmed hat rested on his lap and Smy saw that he was neatly dressed in a grey shirt and linen waistcoat which, although of some many years' usage, were still meticulously clean and pressed.

The man reached into an inside pocket and held out something bronze but dulled with age. "This now belongs to you. It belonged to your father."

It took Smy some time to recover her composure and she was glad that she was still holding the handlebars of her bicycle as it had steadied her when he spoke.

"My father?"

The man nodded. "Here, take it. Like I said, it belongs to you."

Smy leaned her bicycle against the porch wall and took the object from him. It fitted neatly in the palm of her hand and comprised a circular band surrounding the number twelve. Above the band was a castle with three turrets with the central turret surmounted by a small flagpole.

"*Montis insignia calpe.* Latin, obviously. By the sign of the rock?" The man nodded slowly and then quickly looked away.

Smy inspected it once more and noticed at the bottom of the circlet the words 'Suffolk Regiment'.

"It's 'is cap badge. 12th East Suffolk Regiment of Foot. I'd always promised to return it to your mother but I understand she's now gone from us."

"But he died in 1880. It's taken you over thirty years to pass it on to us?"

The man placed the walking stick firmly on the ground for support and raised himself from his seat. "Yes, thirty years and I'm very sorry for not returnin' it earlier. I could lie to you and say that life got in my way - and, in all fairness, that might be true - but I think I secretly liked keepin' it 'cause it belonged to the best man I ever knew."

"Were you with him when he died? All I know is that it was near India."

"Afghanistan. Second Afghan war." The man emerged from the porch into the open sun. He was short but stockily built. It was then that Miss Smy could see the reason for his full beard, noticing that the areas of his cheeks that were visible were indented with innumerable smallpox scars.

"Tell me, Winifred, what d'you know of your father's death?"

"Not so very much. When I was young, my mother told me

that he had died heroically in battle. That it was the 'noble end of a noble life'. She always liked to put it that way. Other than that, she said very little. I think, looking back now, she had little idea how he died."

The slightest of sneers crossed the man's face, which immediately irritated Miss Smy; the stranger didn't fail to notice her reaction.

"I'm sorry. Look, you 'ave 'is badge. I've kept a promise to mysel' even if I was...tardy with the keepin' of that promise. I've one more thing that must be done before I leave these parts. Anyway, that's all by-the-by. Listen, Winifred: afore I go, I want to offer you a choice. As I said, I was there when your father was killed. I can leave you with your mother's view of his death, or I can tell you what really 'appened."

"Surely that leaves me with only one option? After all, if I refused you then I would know that the manner of my father's death was something other than noble."

"Oh, the manner of his death was noble, right enough. You can always carry that fact in your 'eart. And mebbe it is wrong that I suddenly appear out of nowhere and offer the choice I 'ave. But what can I do? There is a truth about the way your father died and I am here to offer you that truth. But you 'ave the right to wish me begone and to walk away this very moment. How old were you when he died?"

"About ten or so. I never did see much of him. I am sure that there are a lot of children whose fathers were in the army who could tell you that."

The man, conscious that the sun was now beginning to beat mercilessly on his head, put on his hat.

"So that's over thirty years, by my reckoning, 'aving lived without acquaintance with the facts. Perhaps it's better left that way."

Miss Smy stopped him from walking away by placing her hand lightly on his arm. "No, don't go. I do need to know what happened."

19

AT MAIWAND PASS

"Let's take a walk around this graveyard. My leg is given' me a fair bit of jip, today. Sittin' don't help none."

"Before you tell me, why were you following me?"

The man stopped and looked at her with surprise. Followin' you? I wasn't followin' you. I was makin' sure I had the right woman. That badge had to go to his daughter and I needed to be sure it was the right daughter. Besides, I think I only saw you the once. Up near the farm."

"But I saw you coming down a field path on the road from Kenton. I was on my bicycle."

He stopped and held his hand up as if waiting for inspiration. Oh, that! That was you was it? Oh no, that wasn't the reason I was there. I was just on my way for a little recce."

"For what?"

But the man deliberately didn't answer and they walked for a little before he began to speak once more.

"Many years ago now, early 1870s, I was in Sudbury at the market. It'd been a good mornin' and we'd sold a good few sheep. Not looking where I was going, I bumped into this man about my age. Good lookin' man too. Taller than me but, as you can see, that wasn't 'ard."

The black and white cat that Smy had seen when she arrived at the church, was now following them both and rubbing itself against the legs of the man and then Miss Smy.

"He apologised even though it were my fault. But there was somethin' about him that I liked and I said that I was just off to wet my whistle at the Olde Bull on Church Street. He'd also done his business for the day so off we went. Of course, we were young men then, although I do remember him tellin' me 'e 'ad a family. We drank too much, he and I, and what do we 'ear when we left the pub but the sound of a drummer! And there was these soldiers, an officer and a couple of sergeants, offerin' the local lads the chance to take the king's shilling. We looked at each other and thought the same thing. Life's 'ard when you're a farm labourer, so why not see a bit o' the world and join up? That's what we were both thinking. Must have been the easiest two recruits that sergeant ever made."

Winifred Smy realised that she still had the cap badge in her hand and, looking once again at it, said, "Suffolk Regiment."

"That's the one. 'Swede bashers' that regiment was known as. Funnily enough, I wasn't even from Suffolk. I'm an Essex man, but what did I care? I couldn't give tuppence whether it were Suffolk or Essex, it was a chance to get out and live a little."

"And did you see the world?"

"Some of it. And I didn't care for a lot of what I saw. But that's army life and your father and I were as close as close could be. A real pal 'e was an' I'll never meet another like 'im."

Smy suddenly remembered the manner by which this man had told her to meet him, and interrupted his recollections with the question, "Whatever made you enter my home the way you did? Why could you have not approached me in the normal way?"

"Because I am going to see you only once and then will disappear. One day you will understand why, but I ain't tellin' you now. Arranging this meeting was the best way I could think of meetin' you 'cause if you were scared o' me - and I do admit I'm not the easiest on the eye - then what better place than an open churchyard? Sanctuary an' all that."

"Before you carry on, where did you find that walking stick? How did you know it belonged to someone I knew?"

The man stopped and turned to Miss Smy, clearly irritated by the digression. "Look, I know who that stick belonged to as I'd seen you walkin' through the grounds of Kenton Hall a few days ago. Where I found it, I'm not going' to tell you 'cause that's not what I'm 'ere for. But I 'ear you're a very smart lady and you'll put two and two together soon enough."

Miss Smy pursed her lips, frustrated at the deliberate way this man could be so open and yet so maddeningly closed. "Please, continue."

"Eventually, 'cause I won't bore you with all the war stories in between, we were despatched to India. Believe me, you don't know 'eat until you've felt the Indian 'eat. Never known anything like it. Couldn't walk across the street without sweatin' like a racehorse after winnin' the derby. Then, one fateful day, your father and I were detailed to accompany the Royal Horse Artillery as they were short of experienced drivers for the 'orses. Little did we realise just what we were walkin' into. But off we went. No choice other than foller orders."

"So were you and my father always together?"

"Thick as thieves, we were. I thought I knew a lot about 'orses, but I couldn't hold a light to what your father knew. I remember once when some wild animal - still don't know what it was - wandered into the camp and frit the 'orses good 'n proper. Your father stood amongst them, calm as you like and took control. 'Orse flesh runnin' everywhere this way an' that. But 'e 'eld 'is nerve and, one by one, 'e got them back under control."

The man shook his head in disbelief, as if still unable to comprehend the act he had just described.

"Anyway, in the July of 1880, we were told that we were all headin' for the Maiwand Pass in Afghanistan and were expectin' to engage with an advance guard of Afghan soldiers. But we were given bad information. It weren't just an advance guard. What we encountered was a fighting force of thousands upon thousands of men. Eventually, despite tryin' to keep 'em back with our field guns, they outflanked us and we 'ad to withdraw. But your father stood 'is ground and drew the Afghan fire so that we could try and get to the wounded and carry them back with us. But there was one soldier who was near where your father was, who wanted to get out of the fight and didn't like what your father was doin'. This coward, 'cause that's what 'e was, seemed to feel that what your father was doin' was endangering everyone. But your father was the only one in danger."

The recollection of the battle stirred something in the man's breast, a heavy emotion that did not allow him to carry on with his story. Winifred Smy became aware of the fact that he was suffering with the retelling, that articulating those long-past events was something he had rarely done before and the feelings that it stirred inside were difficult to keep in check.

"He shot 'im!" the man burst out. "I saw 'im do it. 'E knows I saw 'im do it. It was no Afghan bullet that did for your father, my girl, but one of our own."

"This man shot my father? The man that was panicking?"

"'E knew I saw 'im do it and 'e ran off with the others. I was just about to go after 'im, to kill 'im probably, when I felt this terrible pain in my thigh. Unbelievable pain it was. I'd been shot myself by some Afghan tribesman, and then I blacked out. Woke up in the 'ospital and was told I'd also 'ad my 'ead grazed by another bullet which 'ad knocked me out."

"And this man? The man that shot my father. Did you ever see him again?"

"I've been searching for 'im this thirty years. And now I've tracked 'im down."

"How did you find him?"

The man's manner had changed for the worse and a darkness spread across his face. "Oh, 'e's led me a merry dance, 'e 'as. Changed 'is name twice. 'E knew I was after 'im. First I 'eard that 'e'd gone native for a while in India. Laid low for a long time, but I knew that 'e would have to go back to Blighty one day. I tell you, I went up so many blind alleys over the years tryin' ter find 'im. And then I 'ad a stroke of luck. About six months ago, I'd found myself a nice job at Victoria Station doin' a bit o' porterin'. And then, one day, there 'e was! As large as life. Takin' a load o' suitcases off the train for some family that 'ad just come in from Dover. Everything fell into place after that."

"Do I know him?"

"You do know 'im, so I've 'eard."

"I was told you bought a knife in Debenham."

The man smiled. "No secrets 'round 'ere I can see."

"What have you done with it?"

"Oh, I still 'ave it. It's a nice knife 'n' all. Lost the last one, I did."

They had now reached the gate of the churchyard and Smy could sense that this stranger was ready to leave.

"Who is this man? This man who shot my father. I have a right to know."

"Have I told you my name? No. Have I told you where in the fair county of Essex I live? No. Why? Because when the police start asking questions you will know nothin' of me or this other man but what you 'ave seen 'n' 'eard today. I 'ave kept my strong sense of duty that they drilled in 'ter me in the army. They can 'ang me for what I will do, but I won't be deflected. It 'as been a pleasure meetin' you. You are a right credit to your father. And now I must go."

He raised his hat, opened the gate and walked out onto the High Street. He then stopped and held up his arm as if he had just remembered something.

"Oh, I'm afraid I'm going to do something that will inconvenience you for a little bit. Of course, I apologise for the doin' of it. But, you'll soon be free again. Think of it as 'elpin' out yer ol' man."

"Helping out? How will I be able to help out?"

But the man was already closing the church gate. He raised his stick in acknowledgement of a friendly 'hello' from one of the men from the saddlery who was just taking a short rest, and then - still heavily limping - turned into Gracechurch Street and was gone.

20

A DISAPPOINTING REUNION FOR GASPARD

Once the stranger had disappeared from view, Miss Smy found that her heart felt curiously lighter. The facts surrounding her father's death did not seem to affect her feelings about him. He was - and always had been - a distant figure whose appearance was a rare event in her childhood. She was heartened by her father's courage but it pained her to think that her mother had never truly known the circumstances of his death. No, she decided, it was a long time ago and perhaps she might think differently the more she replayed that day's conversation over in her mind.

And what of the fearful prediction the man had made about exacting revenge for her father's demise? Again, she rationally thought of those that she was closest to and could not think that any of them had anything to do with the events of that now long-distant day at Maiwand Pass.

So why, then, did her mind feel eased? She settled on the fact that this shadow, this skulking threat that she had felt over the last days and weeks had now removed itself and she could turn the full rigour of her intellect to the mystery that was still unresolved: the murder (and she remained utterly convinced still that it *was* murder) of Thomas Eary.

Free now from the tyranny of her recent thoughts, she felt a surge inside that she knew to be a desire for action. She needed to move the opinions of so many towards her own view that the death of Eary was no accident, but that he had been killed through a premeditated and callous act.

She retrieved her bicycle, which was still leaning against the porch wall of the church, and walked down the High Street to the Post Office. Asking for some paper and an envelope, she took her pen and quickly wrote a request before addressing the envelope to Herbert Tranmer at Framlingham Police Station. Knowing that even so modest a town as Framlingham often enjoyed around a dozen or so postal deliveries a day, she was confident that it would reach him in good time.

With a spirit still buoyed by her meeting with her mysterious shadow, Smy cycled back to Kenton with such energy that she managed to negotiate the steep climb and turn immediately after the little hamlet around Red House Farm, a climb that normally demanded her to dismount and walk until the road levelled out again. As she turned onto the Eye Road, she saw Marc-Antoine Gaspard closing the garden gate of her cottage.

"Ah, Mademoiselle Smy. I thought my journey had been in vain but here you are! I had not heard from you since that delightful evening in Kenton Hall and thought I would prevail on you for my walking stick."

"My apologies, Monsieur Gaspard. I have had so much to think about lately that it had completely slipped my mind."

Gaspard affected the slightest of bows. "Apology accepted. You must understand, it is of enormous sentimental value to me. We have had many adventures together."

Smy stood her bicycle against the wall of her cottage and invited Gaspard in. There was a letter which she picked up, briefly glancing at the handwriting on the envelope.

"*C'est une petite maison très charmante.* So clean. And what is this?"

Miss Smy followed his attention which had alighted on a small framed print on the wall. "Oh, that is a drawing of All Saints in Dunwich. I do love the picture. It's by an Ipswich artist, George Frost. Long dead now. I'm afraid the church itself will soon be lost to the sea. It's been the fate of many Suffolk Churches along the coast. Do you like it?"

"Not really. It is too realistic. It is not art but merely a hand-drawn photograph. Art is not there to capture what you can see. Art must be about what you can't see, but you feel to be there." He turned from the picture with a dismissive flourish of his hand and stood before her piano. "Debussy? A tiresome man. The treatment of his first wife was both cruel and scandalous."

"What instrument do you play?"

"Me? I don't play anything. My talents lie elsewhere."

"That's rather unusual. A music critic who doesn't play an instrument?"

"Do you write novels, Miss Smy? I can only think not. But I am sure that you bring a critical eye to the novels that you read."

Miss Smy picked up the letter that had been delivered, held it up and asked, "Do you mind if I open this?"

"Of course not. If you could pass me that glass I will pour myself a little something. I have a horrible suspicion that you might offer me tea and there are only so many abominations one can suffer over the course of one day."

Miss Smy read her letter, occasionally glancing up at Gaspard, who was quite unaware that some of the contents of what Smy was reading related to him. Gaspard sipped on his cognac and closed his eyes with the pleasure of its warming effect. When he opened his eyes it was to behold Winifred Smy standing in front of him with his walking stick.

"I think this is what you came for." She handed him the stick but his initial joy on receiving it was quickly dispelled when he noticed the severe splintering of the shaft. He jumped from his seat.

"What is this? Who has done this to my stick? It is ruined! Why would anyone do such a thing?"

Miss Smy calmly sat down on the piano stool. "When I came home it was lying on my table in the condition you now see. Tell me, Monsieur Gaspard. Where exactly did you lose it?"

"Who found it? That is who should be answering these questions. And why did he do such an awful thing to it?"

"You didn't answer my question."

"But you know who found it?"

"No. I know who returned it. They might not be the same person."

Gaspard grew increasingly exasperated. "Pah! Don't play word games with me. This walking stick is very expensive. It makes me most angry that you return it in such a state."

"When did you first notice that it was missing, Monsieur?"

"Oh, I don't know. I remember going for a walk and when I returned to Kenton Hall, I realised that I didn't have it with me."

Smy lowered her head, knowing that what she was about to say might not be well received. "I find that difficult to understand. You yourself have said that you are inseparable from this walking stick. But it was only when you reached Kenton Hall that you became aware that it was missing."

"What do I care if you understand or not?" Gaspard looked once more at the ruined shaft and shook his head in disbelief.

"Monsieur, you are not all you seem. Today, I find that your *savoir-faire* is skin deep. You have reacted to the damage of your stick in a most infantile way. I did not damage your stick; I merely returned it to you, and you demonstrate a petulance that is most unbecoming."

Gaspard grabbed his walking stick and made to leave.

"No, Monsieur, there is something of the actor about you. And this letter - that I have just received - reveals what I have always suspected."

Gaspard flung back the door and strode out. Smy sat comfortably back in her chair, reached for the unfinished cognac and drank what remained. Only then did it slowly dawn on her that the drink had been poured from a different hip flask to the one that she had first seen in All Saints churchyard.

"Monsieur Gaspard, you really are becoming quite careless."

21

A HOT DAY'S COLD RECEPTION

When Tranmer reached the gates of Grove Hall he looked at his watch before peering down the lane. Eventually, Miss Smy appeared over the brow of a small hill, dismounted expertly whilst the bicycle was still moving and walked briskly towards him. She smiled but he didn't respond, looking rather grim-faced and serious.

"You know that this is very improper. If anyone finds out then I'll be for it and no mistake."

"Did you let Mrs Balthasar know I would be with you?"

"I did, but I'm not sure she believes me. I don't like this one little bit. If it had been anybody else, I would…"

"Yes, yes, Herbert. I'm well aware of the risks you are taking. But I do appreciate it. I just need to spend some time with Melka."

Tranmer sank his hands deep into his trouser pockets. "Why? The poor girl's been through enough, hasn't she? Losing her father like that. She's only a child. And you've still got this mad idea in your head about Eary's death not being an accident. Don't you ever let go of things?"

"Yes, I do let many things go. But I can't let go of the truth."

Smy and Tranmer walked down the long drive that snaked towards Grove Hall. Sturdy oaks and smooth-barked beech trees rose to great heights on either side. There was a slight wind that slithered in small gasps through the higher branches, and the distinctive tap-tap-tapping of an unseen woodpecker emerged from deep within the trees.

Miss Smy was too warm, so she removed her hat and fanned herself with it as she walked along. Reaching the front door, she stood a little behind the Inspector as he pulled the doorbell. A collared dove settled on the path nearby and watched them both with small inquisitive jerks. Eventually, the door was opened by the footman and it was the morose form of Cavenham that stood before them.

"Inspector. Miss Smy. Welcome. You are expected. Please follow me." The last statement was almost said with a sigh, as if the task was a wearying one that must still be executed, however tiresome. They were led into the usual room once more, with Cavenham suggesting that they make themselves comfortable. Neither Tranmer or Smy felt enough at ease to sit down. Tranmer walked slowly along the shelves of books, whilst Smy returned to scrutinise the paintings once more, just as she had done on the very first day she had arrived for her meeting with Mrs Balthasar.

"Curious. Very curious."

"What is?" asked the Inspector, whilst continuing to study the titles of the books.

"These paintings. I noticed it on the first day I came here. When you look closely..."

But the opening of the door interrupted Miss Smy's observation and Mrs Balthasar briskly entered the room. She held out her hand and walked first towards Tranmer.

"Inspector. It's an unexpected pleasure to see you again. And you, Miss Smy. Melka has been asking after you constantly. I'm so glad that we have arranged for you to see her once more."

Smy was taken aback by the warmth of the welcome and found herself smiling whilst trying to comprehend what may lie behind the cordiality of Mrs Balthasar's greeting.

"It is most gracious of you to accommodate me. When the Inspector contacted me to ask if I might be able to walk him through the terrible events of that afternoon, just so that he can be sure that the accident was as he understood it, I also thought it would be an opportunity to return Melka's Algebra book to her and to talk her through my assessment."

"Algebra. Oh, a frightful thing, isn't it, Inspector? I was at a complete loss as a child as to what one might possibly use such a thing for. But I do understand that scientists have found some use for it. But I've no head for science, I'm afraid."

Smy watched Mrs Balthasar's performance, for she knew that that was exactly what it was. Just as with Gaspard the previous day, Smy seemed to be dealing with someone who appeared to slip from one mask to another, and so expertly was one mask exchanged for the next that the real face - the real person - was never revealed.

"Now, let me order some tea and then I will leave you both to it. *J'ai bien peur d'être assez fatiguée cet après-midi.* You simply must forgive my rudeness whilst I go and lie down for a while. Ah, here's Berthe now. Berthe, some tea for these good people please and then be so good as to show them out to the garden when they are ready."

When Berthe returned with the tea tray, she conducted the ceremony with a sullen air, resenting the fact that she should now be treating Miss Smy as a guest. Once she had left, the Inspector poured the tea and asked Miss Smy whether she might like one of the pastries or delicate cakes. Smy refused anything to eat but, after her ride to Grove Hall, gratefully accepted the tea. Tranmer carefully inspected the cakes and pastries and decided on the latter, which he consumed with some relish.

"Very nice. Very, very nice. Are you sure you won't have something?"

Miss Smy smiled and told him no. Tranmer helped himself to a cake this time and ate it with equal enjoyment. Once he had finished, he sank back into the deep comfort of his chair and asked, "So why are we here?"

"Two things. I need to look at the wooded area at the back of the garden. The one that Mr Eary emerged from. The second reason is that I must speak with Melka. I received a letter from her only a few days ago and she is very upset. Not only with the death of her father but the fact that the Balthasars will not permit her to return to her mother."

"Surely that's not an issue you should be concerning yourself with? You're not a member of the Eary family and, to me, Melka is being well looked after by Mr and Mrs Balthasar. If you don't mind me saying, it's very little to do with you."

Miss Smy visibly bridled at the Inspector's words but, remembering that she was now in the house thanks to his assistance, swallowed her pride and said nothing. Berthe re-entered the room and opened the large windows that led out onto the garden terrace. Looking only at the Inspector, she asked, "Shall I clear these things away for you now, Sir?"

Tranmer replied that she should and then asked Miss Smy if she would like to walk outside. Miss Smy turned to Berthe and, having mustered all the warmth in her tone as she could, asked. "Oh, how is your shoulder now, Berthe?"

"It is completely fine now. Thank you for asking."

Smy left the room but could feel the malicious gaze of Berthe burrowing into her back. As they reached the bottom of the stairs that led to the long, beautiful gardens that lay before them, they were joined by Herr Balthasar who was walking towards them, a hunting rifle held in the crook of his arm whilst he lit his pipe.

"Herr Balthasar, thank you for allowing myself and Miss Smy to return."

After puffing at his pipe to make sure it was lit, he slid it to the corner of his mouth. "Not at all. It is a pleasure to welcome you again. Miss Smy, you look as radiant as ever. Melka has missed you greatly."

"I'm looking forward to seeing her, Herr Balthasar. It's good to return, even after that terrible recent event."

Balthasar looked down on his rifle and studied it. "Yes, these are deadly things, aren't they? It's not often they turn on their owner, but one error is all it takes and then it is too late."

Tranmer nodded, knowing that Miss Smy saw the death of Thomas Eary very differently. "Yes, the hunter bizarrely becomes the hunted, Herr Balthasar."

Balthasar grew serious and he looked away to the horizon. "I regret to say, my friends, that we are all about to become the hunted. There are murmurings I have become aware of that, if true, will have catastrophic consequences."

"Surely we will all have the sense to find a solution other than war? Conflict is not inevitable."

"Miss Smy, I only wish you were right. But I was a soldier once. Reasonably high-ranking, as well. I know the minds of soldiers. They can be bold but brittle. Place yourself in the minds of the German people. They feel threatened. They look out from the country and see danger from all directions. Do you expect them to wait until it's too late? No, I may be an Austrian but I know how a soldier, especially a German soldier, sees the world. My only hope is that my beloved Augustus is not drawn into the fight. And believe me, there will be a fight. One last, desperate final fight."

Neither Miss Smy nor Inspector Tranmer knew what to say, and it was left to Balthasar to break the silence. "What am I doing, talking like this? That is not the way to make people feel welcome! Forget my silly talk. 'Wenzel', my wife always says. 'You only see the shadows when the sun shines'. And she's right. Now, go to your business and I will leave you in peace."

But as the two visitors walked across the wide expanse of lawn, both knew that Balthasar's dreadful fears carried more weight than they would care to admit.

22

INTERPRETING THE POKER TELL

"So you want to go into the wood. What for? We've already searched the area and a lot of foliage has already been cleared. You're just wasting your own time and mine."

"And I suspect it's your own time you're most worried about, Inspector. Now let me see. On the day that Eary was shot..."

"On the day he shot himself," Tranmer quickly interrupted.

Smy, standing at the point where the lawn stopped and the first branches of the wood began, let out a long sigh. "When I have proven you wrong, Inspector, you will buy me afternoon tea in Ipswich as an apology."

"And what if I am proven right?" Tranmer smirked.

"But you won't be so your question is a needless one."

Winifred Smy stood amongst the undergrowth and looked carefully around. As Tranmer had said, much of the foliage had been hacked away and Smy grew irritated with herself for not having visited the area on the day Eary had died. She continued to stalk the area, approaching a ten-yard square of ground from different directions.

"What are you doing? Why do you keep walking away and then returning to the same bit?"

Smy looked up and smiled. "We all have our methods, Inspector. Spadger Peck told me a long time ago, that if you look at the same area of ground from different angles you see different things. And Spadger is never wrong about these things. What might be hidden to the eye from one direction, becomes easy to spot when you change to another direction. It's all to do with the way that light falls. Oh, hello..." She crouched down very slowly, anxious not to disturb anything that might cover what she had just eyed.

"Do you remember, last year, when we found the rope in Leucock's Plantation? You may recall that we were meant to find it. And now I have found this - and this I was not meant to find." Smy held up a small silver object.

"What is it?" asked Tranmer.

"It's the lid of a hip flask."

"Well, what of it? Eary wasn't even a man who drank. So what would he be doing with a hip flask?"

Smy inspected the lid, brushed off some earth that had collected inside it and placed it carefully in a pocket. "It didn't belong to Mr Eary. You see..."

"Miss Smy! Miss Smy!" It was Melka, running excitedly across the garden towards them. She flung her arms around her and immediately burst into tears. Looking up Miss Smy realised that Augustus had been asked to accompany Melka and, this office now having been executed, he had stopped a short distance away looking at them contemptuously.

"So, the yokels are reunited. I will leave you here. I have better things to do." With this, Augustus abruptly turned and walked away.

"I hate him so much. He keeps telling me I don't belong here. And he's right. I want to go back to Clopton. I want to see my Ma and my friends. Why doesn't Ma even come to see me? Not once has she been here."

Smy led Melka back out onto the lawn. Tranmer spotted two chairs and brought them over and placed them in the shade. Smy guided Melka to a chair and sat down herself. She reached for Melka's hand and they looked out on the long stretch of grass that ran up to the back of Grove Hall. Large, vibrant pools of colour lay before them from the flower beds that were full of brassy shrubs. Tranmer, sensing that Smy and Melka wanted to be alone, ambled away.

"Melka, I know you don't like Augustus, but what about Mr and Mrs Balthasar? How has it been since I was last here?"

Melka held her hands tight against each side of her face, pushing her features into a distorted shape. "He's all right. Oh, he's very nice and everything. But he's not my Pa."

"And Mrs Balthasar?"

"She tries to be nice, but I hate her. She's the one that's keeping me here."

"How do you know that?"

"Because she does. She keeps saying that this is where I belong and she only took me in because Ma and Pa asked her."

Smy squeezed Melka's hand and watched Tranmer wander from flower bed to flower bed, admiring the fact that - for one who was so often insensitive to some situations - he could still sense when his presence would not be helpful. The wind had now completely dropped and the heat of the July sun had warmed the afternoon so much that even the birds appeared to have fallen into a slumber. A wasp jerked into a space between Smy and Melka, and then slid out of the trees' shadows and into the open.

"Melka, did I ever tell you about something that happened to me when I was a little girl?"

"Only that you lived in Kenton with your mother and she's dead." Melka, with eyes closed, was enjoying this rare moment of intimacy with someone she trusted.

"And so I did. But did I ever mention my father and why he wasn't there?"

"I don't think so. Did you not know your pa? Is he dead as well?"

Smy smiled at the irony of her innocent question, having only just recently become aware of the truth that surrounded his death. "Oh, he's been dead a long time, but that's not what I wanted to say about him. You see, when I was a few years younger than you, he joined the army. He hadn't told anybody that he was going to join, not even my mother. And once he had joined, I hardly ever saw him again."

Melka, taken aback by the sudden turn in the conversation, opened her eyes, sat up and leaned towards Smy. "You never ever saw your pa? That must have been awful."

"Well, I didn't say I never saw him. There were rare times when he would come home. But I was so used to not seeing him that it was strange...strange to see him coming into our house without asking. Strange to see him talking to Mother as if they'd always known each other which, of course, was true. They had known each other a long time."

"Yes, I suppose that must have been a bit rum." Smy could tell that Melka was lost with what she was trying to say.

"The reason I am telling you this is that you think you know things. You think that everything around you is just how it's always been, and then you find out that you've been wrong. I had always thought that it was just my mother and I. But it was never just that. As far as my mother was concerned, it was the three of us: my mother, father and me. It was never just the two of us, as I thought."

"Did you love your pa?"

"No. I pretended I did, but I didn't know him. It's hard to love someone you don't know."

"Yes, I suppose so."

Smy sat on the edge of the chair but still kept Melka's hand in hers. "What I am trying to say is that there are some things in your life that will never change. Our friendship, your love for people who have always looked after you. But, over time, you are going to find out things that will change the way you look at the world. I want you to be brave and trust me. I want you to know that you and I will be friends forever. I want you to realise that, when these things happen, we can eventually adapt and be stronger."

"What else is going to change?"

"When I am confident that I know the truth about everything, then I will tell you the answers to all your questions. When I do, it will be when you and I are on a beautiful beach looking out at the sea. I am going leave you now, but I am promising you that meeting on the beach. A promise from one friend to another."

"Must you go?"

"I must. Oh, and take this." She handed an exercise book to Melka.

"Ah, my algebra book. Just like you said in your note. I burned it, just as you told me to."

"Good. We are a pair, aren't we? You lied to PC Cornish with your letter. I lied to Mrs Balthasar about why I needed to see you. I don't like lying but sometimes the truth demands it."

Melka, who didn't understand Miss Smy's paradox, nevertheless smiled at the conspiracy between them both. "We really are friends, aren't we? Secret friends."

"We truly are. Now, I really must leave. I am going to have a quick word with Augustus and then I will look forward to us meeting on that beach."

"That beach, Miss Smy. Where is it?"

"Oh, you'll soon find out."

"This is for you. I've finished it. Dew yew take it home with you." Melka handed Miss Smy a large rolled-up drawing.

"Why, thank you, Melka." She unrolled the paper and saw that it was Melka's drawing of the house. "Wasn't this the picture you were sketching..."

"When Pa died. I couldn't look at it at first. But then I wanted to give you something because I was so happy that you were coming here. So I finished it yesterday."

"It's beautiful, Melka, and the detail is quite stunning. Thank you."

Melka watched as Miss Smy strode across the lawn and spoke briefly with Tranmer. Then she walked over to where Augustus was sitting reading a book, his feet insolently perched on a table on the verandah that stretched along the back of the great house. Melka couldn't make out the conversation but noticed that Augustus' body language was at first defiant, but then he sat back in a surly acquiescence.

Tranmer had watched the whole episode too although, like Melka, it had been from some distance. As they walked back down the drive from the house, he couldn't contain his curiosity.

"Whatever did you say to Augustus? I thought that he was going to hit you at first."

"Oh, I just told him that if he ever said one bad word about Melka - either to her or about her - then I would tell Herr Balthasar about what I knew he was hiding in his room."

"But what is he hiding in his room?"

"I've no idea. But he's at the age when there is always something prurient to be found in an adolescent boy's room."

"You mean you were bluffing?"

"I believe that it is known amongst the card-playing frater-nity as a 'poker tell'. You unknowingly give away the strength of your hand by signals that you are quite unaware of. Master Augustus, in my short time in Grove Hall, did just that. One just has to know when to play one's hand."

Tranmer laughed and shook his head. "You really astound me, Miss Smy. You really do."

"Do you know what? I have just thought again about the way that Augustus reacted just now. I think there might be much more to be read in that 'poker tell' than I realised."

23

GASPARD CHOOSES NOT TO ABIDE TOO LONG

Although the Reverend Pilbeam possessed a fine speaking voice, his ability to sing did not carry the same distinction. This was much to the chagrin of Mrs Emma Arbon who - rightfully proud of her mastery of the small, rather quirky organ that sat at the back of the nave - scrunched her eyes up in musical agony as Pilbeam's voice filled the small church. The good vicar always began in the right key, but then would flirt with the neighbouring keys before departing on a dizzying exploration of every other key other than the one he had started with. The final chord on the organ and Pilbeam's final note inevitably occupied different musical galaxies.

Once the excruciating dissonance of the final notes had died away, those of a sensitive musical ear were instantly relieved, as if the ropes that had been torturing their bodies on a mediaeval rack had just been slackened for the day.

The church once more provided a milky coolness in which all assembled were happy to bathe. The clouds were doing their best to screen the open face of Suffolk from the sun's fierce heat, but the effort in doing so was now causing them to slowly shred and disappear.

A glance behind told Miss Smy that Gaspard's commitment to church attendance remained undimmed, and he sat once more in the final pew that allowed him a good view of the churchyard through the open south porch door. The service had been underway not fifteen minutes when Gaspard's quiet apology was heard as he asked a parishioner, who was sharing the same pew, if he could pass him. Gaspard then quickly genuflected and rushed out.

Smy looked back but, so quickly had he left, he was now nowhere to be seen. Looking to her right through one of the chantry windows that flanked the south face of the church, she could see him walking quickly towards the Eye Road.

She smiled with a mysterious satisfaction.

Once the service was over, Miss Smy lingered until most of the congregation had dutifully filed out. As before, the Reverend Pilbeam was at the door when Smy eventually left, discussing the choice of hymns with Mrs Arbon.

Seeing Smy, he seemed bent on pulling her into the conversation.

"Miss Smy, do tell this good lady that we ran through 'Abide With Me' with the athleticism of a well-bred colt. I think the great almighty would be heartily displeased that we all seemed quite intent on abiding for as short a time as we could."

"Any slower, Reverend and we'd be rounding on the last verse on Wednesday week. Do you not agree, Miss Smy? Tell the Reverend 'ere you agree."

"I'm with Mrs Arbon. You'd need the lungs of a racehorse if you were to stretch those lines out any longer. Mrs Arbon takes it at a perfect speed and, with all due respect, I would suggest that you would do well to leave all matters musical to our fine organist."

Her honour restored, Mrs Arbon thanked Winifred Smy for her support and walked - head held high - down the church path.

"Well, you're a fine friend! Surely you see my point? There has to be some sense of decorum in our psalmody."

"But it's not psalmody, is it, Mr Pilbeam? It's people who enjoy an uplifting tune and the chance to sing it with a hearty vigour. There's enough to be solemn about at the moment, I think."

"Do you think there will be a war?"

"I'm not sufficiently connected to the powers that be to answer your question. But I am very unsettled by what I read."

Pilbeam grabbed each side of his surplice and fanned the material as if he was cooling himself, but it was a gesture he always did when he was troubled by something.

"Your French admirer briefly honoured us with his presence again, I noticed?"

"My French admirer? I think you're quite mistaken there. I rather feel that I have upset him somewhat, but that was unavoidable."

"Oh, are you still up to your ears with this Eary thing? Detect a little bit of skullduggery, eh? Come inside again and share your thoughts with a poor old priest."

They settled themselves in adjacent pews. "What do you think of Monsieur Gaspard? You've met him at least twice I think."

Pilbeam, still gripping his surplice, looked up at the roof beams as he considered Smy's question.

"What do I think of him? I think he is a perfectly charming

man. I admire his easy manner and he seems very erudite and comfortable with himself. But, if I am honest (and you must vow that this will remain a confidential observation) I can never quite reconcile his actions with his words. A certain incongruence, if you will. Anyway, why do you ask? I believe you asked Mrs Pilbeam the same question."

"A male view occasionally has some worth. To be frank, I believe that he has some involvement with what happened to Thomas Eary."

"Involvement? In Eary's death? Good heavens, that's quite an accusation! Whatever drew you to that conclusion?"

"A combination of suspicion and intuition. As you say, nothing quite fits about him. Can I tell you what first led me to doubt him? It was when we first met outside in the churchyard. I had just finished cleaning my mother's grave when he suddenly appeared. During our brief conversation, he mentioned a couple of things which struck me as odd. For example, he let slip that he knew that Herr Balthasar was living at Grove Hall. Why would he know that? Especially as this was his first visit. And when I pressed him on this point, he tried to convince me that he was sure that Colonel Capon had mentioned Herr Balthasar, and then tried to 'muddy the water' a little, saying that he was perhaps confused because the colonel spoke so quickly."

"And you immediately thought 'That can't be right' because we both know that the Colonel's enunciation is pretty flawless."

"And, if we were to keep this between ourselves, the speed of his speech is in direct opposition to your observations of Mrs Arbon's choice of tempi for your selection of hymns."

Pilbeam winced at Smy's reminder of his earlier irritation. "Yes, quite. But that may just have been a self-deprecating remark, surely. I mean, the man's manners are pretty spot on. You've got to consider that."

"Oh, I have, but my rational assessment of his behaviour still leaves me with some considerable suspicion. And, over time, that suspicion has been further compounded. That is why I asked you for your opinion of him."

"I'm not sure that's fair on the man, Miss Smy. You know how these things go; after an initial doubt is raised, we can begin to cast aspersions on the most innocent actions."

Miss Smy raised her eyebrows but didn't reply. Instead, she gathered her prayer book and rose to leave. "I am a logical person, as you know, Mr Pilbeam. I do my very best so as to not allow emotions to colour my thinking. I have just remembered that I have an immediate appointment outside, if you'll forgive me."

As Pilbeam returned to the vestry to change, Smy walked out into the warmth of the sunshine and looked about. From behind the small holly that had sprung up behind a table tomb at the edge of the graveyard, there emerged a young girl, slight in stature and with a wily grin that lit up her face.

"Ah, it is Lily, my best spy! What did you see?"

"I saw the man you mentioned, Miss. The lovely man with the lovely clothes. So 'andsome!"

"What did he do when he left the church?"

"Why, 'e walked down there and out onto the road, Miss."

"Were you able to follow him?"

"Course. 'E didn't see me. I'm certain 'o that. He met a lady. Posh lady too. Walked away towards Ashfield."

Smy bent down so that her face was level with Lily's. "When you say he met a lady, what was the meeting like? How did they behave?"

"Behave? Why, strange loike. Fust 'e walked fast and then, when 'e got close t' 'er, he slowed roight down. One minute 'e seemed to know 'er. And then it was like 'e didn't know 'er."

"Oh, let me tell you, my little Lily Lambert: he knew her."

24

THE MILL ON THE GREEN

"Oh, yes indeed, if I can pull this story off then I am a made man. My reputation with the editor shall be redeemed and I will be able to marry the girl of my dreams. I am so glad I had the presence of mind to ask for your involvement."

Smy raised an eyebrow at Manners' imperfect recollection. "I distinctly remember that it was I who agreed to your very importunate request that I involve you."

"Hmm? Oh yes, that's just a detail. But here we are again without the inadequacies of the Inspector to waylay us."

Winifred Smy now found herself bridling at Manners' casual dismissal of Tranmer. "There is nothing inadequate about Inspector Tranmer, only the occasional lapse of sound judgement. We are probably all guilty of that, Mr Manners."

But Nigel Manners was one of those irritating people who viewed conversation between two people as a precious opportunity to talk but never to listen. It instantly reminded Smy of her first encounter with Mrs Balthasar who demonstrated the same skewed view of what is necessary when communicating.

That previous afternoon, Miss Smy had received a letter from Manners asking if they might meet up and had proposed the Mill on Saxtead Green as a location, as it was an approximate halfway point between his Framlingham office and Kenton. Although Smy felt that Manners' calculation of the halfway point fell very much in his favour, she had welcomed the opportunity not only to see what news Manners might bring her but to have the chance to exercise by cycling there. The ride had been a pleasant one but the long climb up the hill - as much as any incline in Suffolk might be called a hill - from Earl Soham had proved too much and she had dismounted and walked the rest of the way to their meeting.

To Smy's astonishment, she had found Manners striking the most upright and statuesque of poses. His left hand rested on a walking stick, his left leg before him and his right hand clamped in a fist on his right hip. Rather than be struck by the fact that a man of great achievement - even a god - stood before her, Miss Smy could not avoid the impression that Manners' pose was a perfect imitation of a teapot.

As soon as he had espied her approach, he had relaxed his pose and deigned to enter into conversation. But, as Miss Smy soon found, conversation to Mr Manners was where one invariably realised that all subjects related to him alone. "What a beautiful building! You know, I've cycled or been ferried past this windmill several times but only today have I come to appreciate its magisterial stature. It is a veritable giant that casts its benign yet all-seeing eye over the charming country scene that surrounds it."

Miss Smy sighed in such a way that communicated that she had often had to listen to Manners' purple prose, but such gestures were too subtle to dent his incorrigible self-regard.

But there was no denying the imposing structure that sat just back from Saxtead Green. Its sails were completely at rest and, except for a man nearby who was folding empty sacks in an unhurried manner, the mill seemed very much at peace with itself.

"So, do you have any news, Mr Manners? I am eager to hear what your contacts have told you." She knew that he had something substantial to tell her. Not only because he had summoned her to the spot with his letter, but his head was held higher than normal and his usually gawky limbs seemed - temporarily - to be under control.

"Indeed, I do!" Manners triumphantly returned. "I pride myself on my contacts, all good newspapermen do, and they have come through for me in the most satisfying manner."

"They have come through for us. It was me that furnished you with the intelligence to be pursued."

Manners' vigorous nodding was another act of acquiescence that, to Winifred Smy, was utterly unconvincing.

"Mr Manners, why did I agree to your being involved in the first place?"

"Why did you agree? Because you needed my help. You needed my professional expertise."

Smy cocked her head to one side and weighed up the monstrous ego and indefatigable self-esteem that Manners so effortlessly conveyed. "And the need fell all on my side. Is that what you are saying?"

"I don't quite follow, Miss Smy."

"Then let me orientate you so that you may indeed follow. Not so long ago, in Debenham churchyard, you implored me to involve you because your reputation with your editor was dissolving like snow in summer. And now you assume airs and attitudes that imply that I should deem myself the lucky one. That it has instead been *my* good fortune to assist *you* in resolving the events at Grove Hall."

"Oh, that! My editor? That was just a...just a little spat. I overreacted. Believe me, Miss Smy, my conveyance of that misunderstanding – for that was all it was – was an isolated moment of weakness and one that should be put out of your mind this instant."

Miss Smy stepped back and considered Manners with a considerable degree of mistrust. "Keep your information, Mr Manners, and don't dare to trouble me again."

With long strides and her body leant forward with the sole intention of quitting the scene, Smy was soon picking up her bicycle and pushing it out towards the road. She then turned to face Manners once more. "Do what you will with what you know. But it will be just the merest *hors d'oeuvre* to the *entrée* I intend to lay before the police!"

She placed her bicycle firmly on the road and turned around to Manners once more. "And if one of your morsels of genius is the fact Monsieur Gaspard is not a music critic, well, I've already worked that one out for myself!"

Manners now panicked. It was as if the rope that had been restraining his long limbs had suddenly fallen away and spasms and jerks of arms and legs now beset him. He raised an arm. He covered his mouth. He lifted a leg as if to make haste after her. He then closed his arms and immediately uncrossed them. He turned away and then watched Miss Smy over his shoulder. Both arms were now lifted, like an umpire acknowledging the beautiful six that had just cleared the boundary. But soon, in a dizzying flailing of bone and muscle (such muscle as there was that clung to Manners' bones), he came charging across the green after Miss Smy, shouting her name and imploring her to wait.

Miss Smy had ridden a little way along the road and then slowly squeezed the brakes to stop. If Mr Manners had been able to see her face - which was now hidden from him as she looked over the fields towards Poplar Farm - he would have been incensed to see that it bore a very satisfied smile.

25

HIGH DRAMA ON THE HIGH STREET

It was with some dismay that Winifred Smy noticed the waving arm of George Elwood, who was obviously eager to attract her attention. Once she had reluctantly smiled back to signal her acknowledgement of his wish to waylay her, he pushed past a small group of cows that had been idling their time on the green that ran for a short distance beside Debenham's High Street.

Market Day in the village had now passed its peak; deals had been forged with handshakes accompanied by piercing looks that searched out and interrogated the opposite man's integrity. Nearly all had now made for home or repaired to one of the many pubs that had been waiting to open their beery arms to receive them. The unsold stock remained at various points along the street, watched over by the most junior farm hands or children bribed to police the bleating and the lowing.

"I'm glad I've seen you," said Elwood, smiling. "Saves me the journey up to Kenton."

Striding up towards them both was Mrs Elwood, sharing a memory with an old friend and both laughing at the recollection.

As soon as Mrs Elwood had wished her friend farewell and turned to join her husband and Miss Smy, their faces instantly assumed the same melancholic look which they always wore when in each other's company. Smy, determined not to allow her mood to be changed by the suddenly serious couple, beamed radiantly at both.

"As I said, Miss Smy," George Elwood continued. "It is most fortunate to see you as I understand that Mrs Elwood has a little something to add to our recent conversation. Perhaps you might inquire what that information might be?"

Smy's first instinct was to berate them both for involving her in their highly dysfunctional style of communication but sensing that doing so may result in not hearing Mrs Elwood's intelligence, she decided to nod first at Mr Elwood before turning to hear what his wife might have to say.

But Mrs Elwood merely looked back at Miss Smy, seemingly unaware of what her husband had just said. Smy realised that she would have to play along with the whole charade. For Mrs Elwood to have continued after her husband's conversation would have been an acknowledgement that he existed.

"Mrs Elwood, I hear that you might have something else to relate to me about the christening of Melka Eary."

Mrs Elwood raised her eyebrows in astonishment as if Miss Smy had just read her mind. "Why, yes I do. It's funny you should ask as I was of a mind to write to you as soon as I remembered."

Smy took in a long breath so as not to betray her annoyance.

"I was turning over things in my mind after we last spoke. And as I did so, I realised that I'd not mentioned that there was someone I'd not seen before at that christening. Of course, it might mean nothing, but to me, it felt...oh, I don't know...it felt significant."

"Someone else? Do you know who they were?"

"I know that he was the only one at that christening that I didn't know, Miss Smy. And he sort of stood back as if he shouldn't be there. I remember it all well enough. On the day itself, myself and Mr Elwood had arrived in good time and we stood outside waiting for the Earys to arrive with their little baby. And then, when we all followed the vicar into the church, there he was."

"*He* was?" repeated Smy.

"Indeed. Sitting on the back pew, arms folded and looking like he was expecting us. Funny thing was, the Earys didn't even acknowledge him. And when we stood around the font and the vicar held the baby, well, that's when the strangest thing I ever saw at a baptism happened. It really was the strangest thing, Miss Smy."

"Do go on, Mrs Elwood."

"Well, the vicar asked the Earys what the child's name was to be, and before they had a chance to reply, this strange man came forward from the back of the group and gave the reverend a card. I think he wanted the child to be called 'Bitter'. That's what he said when he handed the vicar the card. I thought you can't call a child that! Thankfully, the vicar agreed and he had a quiet word with the Earys and the child was named Melka. Of course, I would rather it have been a good, solid British name but, thinking about this stranger's first request, I was glad that the Earys settled for Melka."

"And you say you didn't know who the man was?"

"Wouldn't know him from Adam. I think that if you were to ask Mr Elwood the same question, he would say the same."

But Miss Smy had had enough of acting as the communication

go-between.

"Yes, I'm sure he would. This man at the christening. What did he look like?"

Mrs Elwood looked away as she thought. "Oh, it was such a long time ago now, it's hard to remember. A big man he was. And there was something about his clothes. I do remember thinking how nice his clothes were."

So engrossed in her thoughts had Winifred Smy become, that she had failed to notice the small, fat drops of rain that had begun to fall. Her gaze became fixed on a small tussock of grass that had miraculously found a home in a small crack in the road. Yet if Smy instead had been looking down the High Street, then she would have observed three men - two of whom she knew well - walking purposefully towards her. At the head of the triumvirate was Inspector Herbert Tranmer, looking grim-faced and resolute. Behind, trying with all his might to keep up, was PC Cornish. Alongside him was another man, tall and wearing a dark grey suit, the trousers of which he was attempting to not brush against any of the farm animals or their attendant dogs.

The Elwoods, noticing the three men, began to step back, thinking that their objective lay somewhere towards the church, but Miss Smy was their object and they stopped in front of her. Only the proximity of their presence interrupted her deep concentration and she came to with a start.

"Inspector? What brings you to..."

"Miss Smy?"

"Pardon?" Smy's thoughts were fragmented by their sudden arrival and she was momentarily confused as to why Tranmer should be choosing to act so formally with her.

"You know who I am, Inspector. What is this?"

Smy looked over Tranmer's shoulder to see PC Cornish averting his eyes as if witnessing something he wanted no part of.

"Winifred Smy, I am arresting you for the murder of George William Cavenham."

Smy now found her head reeling, unable to take in the unreality of what she was hearing. Tranmer's resolve faltered for a moment, but he collected himself before continuing, "Do you wish to say anything in answer to the charge? You are not obliged to say anything unless you wish to do so, but whatever you say will be taken down in writing and may be given in evidence."

"Cavenham? Murder? What are you saying? What the devil are you accusing me of?"

Tranmer ignored her question and turned to PC Cornish and asked him to disperse the crowd that had started to assemble. Smy felt a hand take a firm hold of her arm as she was quickly led away.

26

THE BODY BENEATH THE BUSHES

"You are an utter imbecile, Inspector!   An utter imbecile!"

Smy walked down Framlingham's Market Hill in such a state of fury that her anger would not allow her the release or satisfaction of crying. In one instance, her need to rid herself of the police station - and all that had just taken place within it - almost caused her to lose her balance as the toe of her shoe stubbed against a flagstone that was not flush with its neighbours. On she hurriedly strode, only gradually becoming aware that the sheer exertion of her walking was causing her to perspire uncomfortably.

"Miss Smy!" Tranmer was trying to walk and scamper in short, alternating bursts. It was a vain attempt to balance two needs: the first to maintain some decorum which he felt was expected of a man of the East Suffolk constabulary; the second was to try and catch up with the fast-receding Miss Smy. It was only when he had collided with a woman carrying fruit to the market, and then stopped to help her pick up the scattered contents of her basket, that he gave up on his quarry. The

145

woman carrying the fruit, once she was happy that nothing had escaped, gave him such a withering look of disdain that Tranmer had to quickly - and rather shamefacedly - look away.

Tranmer had had the worst of days. A call had arrived at the police station that morning to say that a second death had been perpetrated at Grove Hall. Tranmer was dispatched along with Inspector Sibley, a colleague whom he despised but had been made to work with by his superior, Superintendent Freeman. When they had finally arrived at Grove Hall, it was to be met by an ashen-faced Herr Balthasar, who walked with them to the side of the house.

A high, long perimeter wall was hidden from view by a variety of large bushes and small trees. It was there, as Balthasar carefully explained, that he had seen his dog, Claude, repeatedly enter. "That was just so unlike him," Balthasar had explained. "He never fails to come whenever I call him. But, eventually, he wouldn't come out and so I went in to find him."

Some 30 or 40 yards away, they could see both Mrs Balthasar and Augustus, standing together; she had placed her hand on his arm as if to stop him from going any nearer, although there seemed to be no signal on his part that he wanted to see the grisly scene.

The two policemen nodded to one another and pushed aside the branches that flicked back into their faces, trying to make their way through to where the body lay. The first thing they noticed was the swarming of flies both on and around the corpse, grimly gorging themselves on any area of exposed flesh. Once temporarily satisfied, they would circle the small space for a few seconds before returning to their ghastly feasting. Tranmer and Sibley tried to swat away the flies that had turned their eager attention to the interlopers, drawn to their warmth and smell.

Tranmer took a handkerchief from his pocket and covered his mouth, worried that he might swallow one of the irritating assailants. He crouched down and heard, from over his shoulder, Sibley's voice declare, "My stars, just look at that!" It wasn't the body, stretched supinely on its back, that caused Sibley's outburst. Rather it was the sleek, curved sword that seemed almost to pin the corpse to the ground, so deep had the blade been thrust into the dead man's chest. The eyes of the long white face were open as if death had suddenly stolen upon the man only moments before. His hands were raised and the stiffened fingers all pointed to the blade that was erect between them.

It was Sibley, who noticed something else that only became apparent upon closer inspection. The dead man's mouth was slightly open, and through the small gape Sibley could see that a ball of paper, scrunched into a tight roll, had been forced into the mouth. He went to extract it but it was Tranmer who told him to wait. "Let the photographers do their bit first. Don't move or touch anything."

"But I won't move anything," Sibley replied petulantly.

"Bide your time. You know the rules."

It was Balthasar's voice, who remained out on the path, that broke their concentration. "Inspector, I think some of your colleagues have arrived also. Shall we ask them to wait?"

Tranmer stood up as much as the heavy foliage would allow and returned to Balthasar, leaving Sibley with the body. It was not only the police photographer, carrying just the sort of equipment that they would soon find almost impossible to use in such a confined space, that was walking slowly towards them. Behind him came the rapidly shuffling feet of a small, thin man whom Tranmer knew to be a local doctor.

Tranmer greeted both and was just about to convey the details of the cramped space that they would have to negotiate, when the excited figure of Sibley emerged onto the path, clutching a sheet of crumpled paper in his hand. "Look! Look at this, Tranmer!"

Tranmer was momentarily confused and looked down at the document that was being offered to him.

"What is it? Hang on, where did you get that, Sibley? Was that the paper that was in the dead man's mouth?"

Sibley turned his back on the others and conspiratorially lowered his voice. "It was. Look at it. Don't worry about protocol and all that rot. We can soon stick it back in the old fellow's gob."

Tranmer, his interest in Sibley's plunder now piqued, quickly pointed out how the photographer and doctor might best gain access to the body and then took the other Inspector aside. "Let me have a look at it."

Tranmer immediately recognised it as a death certificate, but what first drew his attention was the name 'Smy'. Closer inspection told him that it was the death certificate of a Daniel Smy, showing the date of death as 27th July 1880. But the location of the death surprised him most, for it read, 'Maiwand Pass, Afghanistan.' Yet more curious still was the column that was headed 'Cause of Death', for the original entry had been defaced so much that it was impossible to make it out. Next to the column, someone had neatly written 'murdered by a cowardly swine from the regiment of the Royal Horse Artillery.'

"What do you think?" interrupted Sibley. But Tranmer chose not to reply and gave a slight shrug of annoyance.

"Turn it over, Tranmer."

"Hmm?"

"Look at what's on the other side."

Tranmer turned the certificate over and read, "I have now avenged my Father." He tried to take in this fresh information but struggled to do so. Little by little, scraps of conversation returned to him and it was always Miss Smy's voice that he heard. He particularly remembered one conversation (was it only earlier this year?) where she had responded to his questions about her family. And now the scraps of information started to form coherent strands. The army father she barely knew. The all too few letters that her mother would cherish and allow to let fall from her stubby fingers as she fell asleep. Her 10-year-old self coming to terms with her father's death and her mother's unquenchable grief. The small, beautifully carved cedar box that her father had once bought in a Kandahar market that had been sent back to her after his death...

And so the events of the day had rapidly run their course and a meeting back at Framlingham police station had come to one conclusion, one that Tranmer found himself fighting to resist. But Superintendent Freeman's direction was unequivocal: Miss Smy was the obvious murderer and must be apprehended as quickly as possible.

Tranmer, still unable to accept that it was Smy who had carried out the murder, found himself walking up Debenham High Street with Sibley and PC Cornish in tow. Sibley, utterly convinced that they were about to apprehend the murderer, Tranmer and PC Cornish trudging up the hill like two men walking towards the gallows, quite unable to believe her capable of such an act.

Yet it was Smy's face, the image of her shocked and hurt expression, that he couldn't seem to clear from his mind.

Sibley's face bore the triumphant satisfaction of a case having successfully been solved. Tranmer's face conveyed only a terrible feeling of a deep betrayal.

27

SIBLEY MEETS HIS MATCH

"Cavenham? The butler, Cavenham?"

"I believe you knew him, Miss Smy? Not only knew him but worked closely with him."

Miss Smy had looked at the wall and repeated the name as if it was new to her. Sibley interpreted this as a desperate attempt to buy time for herself and that his interrogation was working.

"Come come, Miss Smy. It all hangs together rather nicely, doesn't it? You went to work for Mrs Balthasar because you knew that this man had once known your father in the army. Why, it gave you the perfect reason to get close to him, learn his comings and goings, and establish the ideal time that you might kill him."

"Why would I want to kill Cavenham? I'd never met the man before I worked at the Balthasar's house. I never liked the man - in fact I deeply loathed the man - but I would never take the life of another human being."

"Well, Inspector Tranmer and I were hoping that you would give us the last piece of the jigsaw. According to our records, or the records kindly supplied to us by the Suffolk Regiment, they were both present at the battle of…now, where was it…"

"Maiwand," added Tranmer, who appeared unconvinced by the whole procedure.

"And with this sword…" Sibley walked over to a table at the side of the room and took out the weapon from under a large grey cloth that had been covering it.

"Recognise it?"

"I have never seen it before. I don't even know what sort of sword it is."

"As I think you well know, it's the sword of an Afghan tribesman. Many were brought back from the second Afghan wars by our brave soldiers. Your father may - or may not - have told you that it is known as a Pulwar Sword. A beautiful, if very deadly, thing. I do suggest to you that it belonged to your father. Where did you keep it? In your house, perhaps?"

It was indeed a beautiful weapon. The handle of the sword was topped by a bud-like finial, and the hilt was engraved with delicate flower heads. Towards the top of the long steel blade was a brass crescent moon that shone whenever the sword caught the light coming through from the small window.

"I tell you under any oath you care to bring me, that I have never seen that sword before." And then, as she repeated her innocence, everything suddenly fell into place for Winifred Smy. Why had she not seen it all earlier? Probably because her shock at being arrested and then hearing once again that it was Cavenham that she was supposed to have murdered had scrambled her thoughts. But now the conversation in the amongst the graves of Debenham's St Mary Magdalene's church came back to her.

So it was Cavenham who had killed her father over thirty years ago. He was the coward who, in a desperate act to preserve his own skin, had shot the man who was drawing the attention of the marauding Afghan soldiers to their unit, in order to save the precious guns that the British army were trying to retrieve. And this man in the churchyard - of course, she had never found out what his name was - had exacted his revenge all of these years later. And what was that he had told her before she saw him walk away? Wasn't it something like, "I'm going to inconvenience you for a little bit..."

Smy felt her defiant spirit rise and she instantly turned to Sibley and asked, "What time did the doctor say that Cavenham was murdered?"

Sibley felt on the back foot as she snapped out the question. "The time...oh, he thinks afternoon to late evening..."

"Miss Smy," Tranmer rose from his chair as he spoke. "Where were you yesterday evening between, say, 3.00 pm and 11.00 pm?"

"I'm glad you asked, Inspector. I think you will find that Mrs Chevallier will account for my presence from 1.00 pm - when we both enjoyed a very good luncheon - until 6.00 pm when I had to make a reluctant leave-taking."

Tranmer took the sword from Sibley, held it up in front of his face so that the blade was pointing away from him and viewed the curve of the blade with one eye closed.

"And after you left Mrs Chevallier's?"

"I walked from Aspall Hall to Kenton and helped decorate the church for Polly Gooding's wedding this Saturday. Both Mrs Pilbeam and Polly's mother can vouch for my presence in the church that evening, I'm certain. Afterwards, Mrs Pilbeam insisted that we return to the vicarage to enjoy some refreshment and it was, if I remember correctly, almost 11.30 in the evening before I left with Mrs Gooding."

Sibley sucked in his cheeks and casually threw back, "Well, I will need to corroborate that, I'm afraid. Up to this moment in time, you are our chief suspect and will remain so until proven otherwise."

"Oh corroborate away, Inspector Sibley. I would expect nothing less than your continuing infatuation with bureaucracy. And whilst we are setting the record straight, it was Mrs Balthasar who asked me to apply for the position of Governess, not the other way around as your earlier fairy story suggested. I had no idea that the Balthasars had recently taken up residence at Grove Hall so would not have had any knowledge of who their butler was." She turned her eyes to Tranmer and he caught a flash of deep indignation.

"Am I free to go?"

"Yes," said Tranmer. "But you must inform us of your whereabouts at all times in case we need to speak with you again."

"I think you know where to find me, Inspector Tranmer. Please show me the way out. I have rather a longing to breathe in some unpolluted air."

Tranmer escorted Winifred Smy through the building and out onto the still-bustling Market Hill. It was now after 8.00 pm and the stalls of the various market traders were long closed although some were still restocking their wares ready for the next day.

"Look, Miss Smy, I had no choice..."

"Leave me alone, Inspector. How could you even think that I...you've even been a guest in my own house!"

"I don't for one moment..."

"Leave me alone. To think that someone whom I have known for so many months would think such a thing of me. You are an utter imbecile, Inspector! An utter imbecile!"

That was how the whole, long day had unfolded for Inspector Tranmer. It had been a day of high surprise and deep embarrassment. In that one day, and it was not finished yet, he felt he had run the full gamut of emotions. A hand was rested on his shoulder and he turned to see the shifting limbs of Nigel Manners before him.

"Ah, it's you." Tranmer's voice faltered.

"It certainly is! You see before you the happy betrothed. I am now officially engaged and Miss Beatrice Bartholomew is to be the lucky woman to claim my undying marital devotion."

"Oh yes, of course, congratulations."

"Now look here, old man. I know that Miss Smy rather hoped that it would be to her that I would romantically incline to, but I don't hold with that sort of older woman thing. But, now that I, the great press gladiator, have withdrawn from love's arena, might I suggest that you set your trident and net for Miss Smy yourself. What do you think, old man?"

"Oh, for pity's sake, Manners, you...you imbecile!"

28

AN APOLOGIA

Of all the gardening activities that Miss Smy found comforting, it was weeding between the rows of vegetables that she enjoyed most. It always produced a calmness that filled her as water fills a ewer and, in time, so lost in the labour did she become that any residual anxiety she still had gradually ebbed away.

She replayed the events of the previous day repeatedly at first, unpicking each moment as if it had been a stitch in a patchwork of memory. But it was the thoughts about the gruesome death of Cavenham that constantly interrupted her rumination, and the fact that she had unknowingly been working - albeit for such a short time - with the man who had killed her father.

Was there something telepathic that contributed to her instant dislike of the Balthasars' butler? No, she concluded, he had been a wizened stalk of a man, a hollowed-out human being, a person void of any feeling, sensitivity or emotion. The fact that he had killed her father so many years ago was due to yet another defect in his character: to be such a coward that he would willingly sacrifice the lives of others to save his own empty skin.

From where she knelt she could see the tower of the church and watch the ever-changing shapes of the grey-white clouds that crept behind it. A robin flew from a nearby rose bush onto the handle of her basket, which was only three or four feet away. Its inquisitive look seemed to be asking of her 'What troubles you so much?' Smy grinned at the audacity of the creature and stood up, her mind now turning to thoughts of breakfast.

It was as she was walking back to the house that a question leapt into her mind: 'Am I an accessory to a murder?' She could not be anything but completely honest with herself. She had known that her father's friend was bent on avenging his death and he had told her that it was someone she knew, but what could she have done? If she'd reported the potential crime to the police, would they have taken her seriously? And, even if they had, could they have been expected to individually guard every male that she knew in the county? Even if she had informed them, they would have had to find and restrain him, but for what? He could have easily passed off his conversation with Miss Smy as merely the ramblings of a man prone to revealing the inventions of a fevered imagination.

No, she concluded, it would have been fruitless. Nevertheless, she resolved to tell the police all that had happened once she had finally untangled the other matter troubling her mind: the shooting of Thomas Eary.

Once breakfast - which was only a little bread washed down with strong tea - was over, she thought about cycling to Debenham but, with the ignominy of yesterday's events, decided that it would be too awful an ordeal to face. The click of her letterbox told her she had post and she picked up the letter that now lay in the hall. She grimaced as she looked at the envelope, instantly recognising Tranmer's distinctive handwriting. At first, still in high dudgeon, she threw it onto the kitchen table, determined not to read it. But, as the first fierce flames of her anger subsided, she sat down and opened the letter.

My dearest Miss Smy

You may never open this letter; you may never even acknowledge to me that you have read this letter; yet, I really do hope that you give me a chance to explain the awful events of yesterday to you.

I can't quite remember where I first encountered it, but I have always liked a George Bernard Shaw quotation which runs, 'When a stupid man is doing something he is ashamed of, he always declares that it is his duty.' Yesterday, despite my pleading the opposite, I was forced to arrest you. The fact that I had to be accompanied by the loathsome Sibley only added to my extreme discomfort. I was convinced that, as much as you had once told me that you despised Mr Cavenham, you were a woman of the highest integrity and could never have resorted to such an act, even to the point of avenging your father.

I had suggested that Sibley lead the questioning because I could not bring myself to do it. Both he and Superintendent Freeman know of my association with you (I personally would like to have thought of it as a friendship, as we so recently agreed it was) and I believe that Superintendent Freeman saw it as a test of my impartiality.

Writing this letter to you is unwise – and unprofessional – of me, but I do so in an attempt to let you see that it was not my doing.

Having written the above, I cannot tell you how sorry I am for the way that this dreadful event must have affected you and your memories of your father. To have died whilst serving your country is a noble act, but to have died at the hands of your own kinsman would make any decent man or woman's blood boil.

I will leave the matter there. I hope I have, to a little extent, enlightened you about my behaviour. I do sincerely wish that we might resume our friendship once more.

Sincerely

Herbert Tranmer

"A woman of the highest integrity? I rather think not." said Miss Smy, aloud. If she was a woman of such integrity, would she have not tried to reason with Cavenham's killer? As futile as she had told herself it would have been, had it not been her duty to immediately go to the police with the details of that fateful conversation in Debenham churchyard? Was it not incumbent on her now to go immediately to the police station and to impart all that she knew about the...

...she couldn't use the word 'murderer'. It was the correct word in the eyes of the law, but she was too close to the emotional centre of the act. Was it really murder? Or was it an act of revenge that balanced the account in the mind of her father's friend? How did the biblical verse put it? *'And if any mischief follow, then thou shalt give life for life, eye for eye, tooth for tooth, hand for hand, foot for foot, burning for burning, wound for wound, stripe for stripe.'*

This satisfied her somewhat and she lay the letter aside. But then she remembered a sermon that the Reverend Pilbeam had once given about why such acts of revenge were abhorrent. What was the verse he quoted on that Sunday morning? It was Matthew, Chapter 5: *'Ye have heard that it hath been said, an eye for an eye, and a tooth for a tooth: but I say unto you, that ye resist not evil: but whosoever shall smite thee on thy right cheek, turn to him the other also.'*

Closing the front door behind her, Miss Smy mounted her bicycle and set out for Framlingham Police Station.

29

A CALL FOR HELP

"Matthew! Matthew, Chapter 5. Verse…Verse 37 or 38, I think. How awful, a priestly man such as myself in want of a bible. Oh well, no matter. The act was the thing. Something like, I say unto you, that ye resist not evil… Err…what was it again? But whosoever shall smite thee on thy right cheek, turn to him the other and so on and so forth. Oh yes, Miss Smy, you did the right thing."

"Well, it's good of you to say that but I can't seem to convince myself that it was the right thing."

The Reverend Pilbeam closed the lid of the organ and checked that all of the stops had been closed. "I'm not sure that there always is 'the right thing'. Sometimes we do the best thing and live with that as our choice. You say that the police were very understanding?"

"Inspector Tranmer was very understanding. I can't speak for the entire force, unfortunately. I have given them a full description but he could be anywhere by now. Of course, that's why he left the evidence that made it look like I was Cavenham's nemesis. All efforts were directed towards me which I am sure gave him precious time to be well away from the county. I'm also certain that he even purchased the knife in Abbots as a deliberate red herring. If he'd used that to murder Cavenham then it would have implicated him immediately. As it was, he had always known exactly what he would kill Cavenham with. A murder weapon with a very particular significance."

Pilbeam, still seated on the organ stool, leant forward and asked, "Are you all right, Miss Smy? You know, this must all have been a terrible ordeal for you." Winfred Smy moved away from the pew she had been leaning against and reached for her hat. "Yes, I think I'm all right. Tell me, have you seen Gaspard lately, the Frenchman staying with Colonel Capon?"

"He's certainly not blessed us with his presence at church since last Sunday. Unless he has returned to *la belle France* I would think we might well see him at Colonel Capon's little *soirée* on Saturday. Mrs Pilbeam and I will be leaving the vicarage at five o'clock, should you care to accompany us to Kenton Hall?"

"I would like that. I'm looking forward to going."

Pilbeam and Smy walked out into the late afternoon sun and stood in the churchyard in silence; she always felt somehow comfortable enough in the Reverend's company that conversation was not always required.

He reached for his pocket watch and checked the time. "Oh, I think I must be returning or I will be late for lunch. Can I ask you something before I go? It's a little impertinent really, but as the person responsible for his flock I feel I have some right to ask. Why have you been coming to church lately? I had you down as a rabid unbeliever, but have been delighted to see you join us. Has there been some Damascene moment that has returned you to the fold?"

Winifred Smy quietly laughed and shook her head. "I'm afraid not. Perhaps it's nothing more than the 'bells and smells' as the Catholics like to say. No, I rather think that there's some unspoken need that urges me to go. And I love the church, as you well know. I suppose that now I am on my own, to sit with the kith and kin of the parish gives me the succour of company which even the most retiring of us finds a blessing."

"A blessing? When you use language like that, I think you *are* a secret believer. Mark my words, you will return to us one day, body, heart and soul."

Smy was just about to tell him that he would be sorely disappointed when seeing that his face was so full of hope that his prediction would come true, she found that she didn't have the heart to contradict him. After they departed, Smy walked down the church path, out onto the Eye Road.

It was the sound of a motor car approaching from behind that caught her attention. As it slowly drew to a halt beside her, she immediately recognised the creamy bodywork of the Balthasars' car. A rear door opened and out stepped Berthe, this time not as frosty in her attitude as she had previously been.

"Good morning, Miss Smy. I trust I find you well?"

"You do indeed. And you?"

"Quite well, thank you, under the circumstances."

"Yes. It was an awful thing to have happened to Cavenham. How is Melka?"

"That is why I was sent for you. I'm afraid that Melka is not at all well. Mrs Balthasar is at quite a loss as to what she should do. Her husband suggested that it might be wise to call on you. If you are free, could I ask you to come with me to Grove Hall? I would perfectly understand if you are too busy to attend."

Miss Smy considered the offer for some seconds. There was

a deep reluctance to appear to be available at the whim of Mrs Balthasar, but the thought of Melka's distress over-rode any personal pride she had.

"Of course. I would be happy to help if I can."

It was only a matter of ten minutes or so before the car was pulling into the drive of Grove Hall. Berthe and Winifred Smy stepped out with Berthe showing her intention that she should follow her to an entrance at the rear of the house.

"I don't think so. I came here not as an employee of this house, but as a guest. I think, therefore, that the front entrance would be more appropriate."

Smy could see that Berthe was incensed by her request but she acquiesced all the same and it was through the front door that Miss Smy entered the hall. Once again, Miss Smy found herself in the same room that she had first been shown into, seeking the governess position.

Berthe left the room but it was not long before the door was again opened and Herr and Mrs Balthasar entered. It was Mrs Balthasar who spoke first.

"Miss Smy. It's so good of you to come so quickly. First, I was afraid that you might not be found and, second, I feared that you might be too busy to come to us straight away."

"When I heard that Melka was not well, I could hardly refuse."

"Nevertheless," said Herr Balthasar, "it is deeply appreciated. My poor wife has been very affected by all that has happened. The murder of Mr Cavenham and now Melka's strange mood."

"So Melka is not ill?"

"It all depends on what you mean by 'ill'. She refuses to speak to me or my wife. She has become quite distant. Neither of us can get a single word from her. And now she refuses to eat."

"Will you talk with her?" pleaded Mrs Balthasar. "You are

our only hope."

Miss Smy thought for a moment, looking from one strained face to another. "I will speak to her on one condition, that you accede to a request that I will make of you."

Mrs Balthasar was the first to answer. "A request. What sort of request?"

"A reasonable one. Say yes and I will let you know what the request is. Say no, and I will leave your house immediately."

"Surely all you need to do is to try and speak to her!" Herr Balthasar's voice grew more agitated as he spoke.

"Yes or no? I need only one answer."

"For the sake of the child, yes. You have my word."

"Thank you, Mrs Balthasar. My request to you both is this..."

30

THE LIMPING MAN LIMPS NO MORE

"Where did you find it, Spadger?"

"The Great Wood. Up near Crows Hall. Asked around o' course. A word here. A word there. People always notice. I wuz talken to ol' Billy Cocksedge. 'E saw 'im a couple o' times, 'e said. Funny cove, he thought. Saw him twice up by Nuttery Belt. Fust time with a stick. Second time, no stick."

Smy laughed. "So this stick was just a prop. A little bit of theatre to make us think that he could never move very fast because his limp was so bad."

"Thas about the size o' it. Course, that's what you told the constabulary, an' thas what they will 'ave told every constable to look out for. An ol' man with a limp an' a stick. Accorden to Cocksedge, this fella wuz allus 'aven' us on. Wily, eh?"

Smy poured some more beer into Spadger Peck's glass; he made no pretence to refuse her generosity and his face always settled into its usual easy repose. It was that facial 'easy repose' that had served him so well over the years, especially when policemen - who ought to have known better - laid various accusations before him. Smy knew that that look of childish innocence hid a thousand misdeeds but who could ever hold him to account? Over the many years, she had heard others speak about how untrustworthy he was, and yet she had cemented a relationship with him that was unfailingly faithful. One had never lied to the other, although Smy knew full well that Spadger's truths were often economically communicated to her.

"You know, Spadger, I would have liked to have talked with this strange man more. To have found out something more about my father. I was young when he was killed. I have spent my life hearing my mother's heroic stories of him and yet, as always, the truth is maybe a little bit disappointing. He was as ordinary as the rest of us."

"The truth allus is disappointing. I knew your father an' when I listen to you, I am listenen to 'im. 'E had your principles, n' 'e 'ad your temper. But 'e never 'ad your tolerance. I wuz wary of 'im and 'e wuz wary o' me. I liked 'im, but I didn't care for 'is company."

Smy sat back and considered Spadger's musings. "Do you think he was on to you, Spadger? Knew what career you were planning for yourself."

"Career? Why, Miss Smy, I detect a judgement in your opinion and I don't care for it! I'm a God-fearen man an' no mistake. Honest as the day is long."

"But what about the nights, Spadger? Isn't that where most of your career is spent?"

He threw his head back, banged the table with his beer mug and laughed loudly at the observation. "Dew yew stop your accusen, Miss Smy. A man is not guilty until proven so!"

Winifred Smy leaned forward and rested her head on her

hands. "Spadger, you told me that you didn't think Thomas Eary was capable of making such a mistake as to shoot himself with his own rifle. Do you remember telling me that?"

"I do. An' there's another thing that occurred to me after that conversation. Such a thing as I kicked myself for not thinken o' it afore."

"Tell me."

"Well, why would 'e be in those woods at the back o' Grove Hall with 'is gun? Makes no sense. 'Cos..."

"Because it's not the hunting season! Of course! No one starts hunting until mid-August."

"Thas zactly it, Fred. Ol' Charlie wouldn't 'ave been hunten. It's not the season."

"I knew it, Spadger! I knew that there was something wrong with that shooting. An accident, they told me. That was no accident. There was another reason why I knew he'd been murdered. Something that the police seemed to quite overlook."

Spadger was so taken by Smy's outburst that his glass hovered at a point midway between the table and his lips. "Another reason, Miss Smy. What other reason?"

"Well, when we turned the body of Mr Eary over, I noticed..."

A sharp rap on the door interrupted their conversation. She left the table and went out to see who the caller was, fearing it would once again be Berthe eager to usher her back to Grove Hall.

She opened the door to find Augustus Balthasar standing outside. The first feeling she experienced was one of revulsion, but she noticed something she'd never seen in him before, an expression of contrition.

"Oh, hello." was all she could muster in that moment.

"Miss Smy. I would very much like to speak with you. Of course, if this is not convenient..."

"Well, I do have a friend here. Come in." Smy led Augustus into the kitchen and, to her astonishment, she found that Spadger had disappeared. His glass, expertly drained, remained on the table but no other sign that he had ever been present was there.

Smy, somewhat embarrassed, turned to Augustus Balthasar and offered a weak, "Oh, he seems to have left."

When Smy had first met Augustus, he seemed to be the very embodiment of all that is worst in the adolescent: a body that is changing faster than the mind can cope with; the total belief that one's own opinions are not only right but at such a lofty height that they are above contradiction. With Augustus, one had to add an unpleasant sense of brooding violence although - to see him now - standing so awkwardly in Miss Smy's kitchen, was to see a very different young man.

Winifred Smy observed him closely. There was no hint of malevolence, no desire to assert his superior station. Yet she remained watchful, well aware that this was the spiteful boy who had spiked her tyre.

"Melka's left. Did you know that?"

"Yes, I knew that. I'm sure that's an arrangement that you're more than comfortable with."

"I know what you're thinking. You're thinking I was rather beastly to her. Well, I was. I don't mind telling you that I was jealous. I knew nothing about her. And then, when we got to Grove Hall, all the talk was about this Melka. Always Melka. I know that my step-mama was her godmother, but why would she want her to live with us? And then when I met her..."

Augustus' face told Miss Smy everything that was seething

inside him: his innate snobbery; his sense of entitlement; his despising those less fortunate in their situations.

"Have you come all this way to tell me how terribly you've been treated? I have so many other things to do with my time."

Augustus Balthasar hung his head and sat down in the same chair that Spadger Peck had been occupying. "I'm a disgrace, aren't I? A sad, privileged disgrace. Despise me, Miss Smy. Oh, I deserve it. Despise me. But let me ask something of you: please help my father. He is wrestling with something and I don't know what. Ever since Melka's father died he has been... unsettled. Different. I went out shooting with him some days ago - this was before old Cavenham was killed - and he couldn't have hit a pheasant if it had been one yard from the barrel of his gun. This is the very same man who was the most accurate shot in the Imperial Austrian *Landwehr*."

Smy folded her arms and walked around the edge of the room. "Whatever made you think I would be able to help him? I have my limits, young man."

Augustus looked up and stared at Winifred Smy with wild eyes. "Tell him to admit to what he's done. Tell him to stop the pretence and admit to what he's done!"

Smy opened the door that led out to the hall and stood aside, giving a clear signal to Augustus that the conversation was nearing its close. "I will think over what you have just told me. Can I ask you something? Have you all been invited to Colonel Capon's garden party on Saturday?"

Augustus Balthasar was somewhat taken aback by the change of subject. "Garden Party? Why, yes. I believe so."

"Just one other thing, and it's a silly question to ask, I know, but when Mr Eary was killed, where were you?"

"Where was I? In my room of course. I have a lot of reading

to get through before I return to my school."

"Had you been there since breakfast?"

"I believe so. Why are you asking?"

"Forgive me, Augustus. It's just something that has been bothering me, but I'm glad to say that your answers have greatly settled my mind. You may leave now."

31

THE GUESTS ASSEMBLE

It had been a very warm day but, thankfully for Colonel Capon's guests, a thin gauze of clouds had unfolded itself across the sky and everyone felt the more comfortable for it. Colonel Capon continued to hold the summer garden parties that his wife had started many years ago. His wife, now dead for only a few years, loved to entertain and, when the weather permitted, she particularly loved that any event should take place outside. The tables, with the corners of their virgin white cloths lifted occasionally by a lazy wind, were arranged around the beautiful knot garden that lay at the front of the house, separated from the building by one side of a deep moat. In between the box hedging had been planted herbs and other aromatic plants, all releasing their generous fragrances to the visitors.

The Chevalliers, long-standing friends of the Capons, had yet to arrive which accounted for the furtive glances towards the avenue from the Colonel's household. As soon as the Colonel registered that Mr and Mrs Pilbeam had arrived with Miss Smy, he excused himself from the conversation he was having with the effortless charm of the seasoned host.

"Good afternoon to you all! It is delightful to welcome you. Mrs Pilbeam, you really ought to release yourself from this dreadful man and marry me. We could have a party like this every day."

"But what about my wife's spiritual sustenance, Colonel?" replied the vicar. "If she was married to you, then all my hard work would be undone."

"Yes, I'm afraid you're right, vicar. How about you, Miss Smy? You're so much younger than an old curmudgeon like me. One day, all this could be yours!" Unfortunately, the very same hand that had indicated to Miss Smy the full extent of his property also happened to be holding a glass of wine, and a shriek from a young servant girl who was passing behind the Colonel at that moment told him that some of the contents had landed on her.

"My dear Mary, I'm most awfully sorry. Are you very wet? No? Oh, you couldn't just recharge this glass then. You are a dear."

The Colonel looked back at his guests and offered a childish grin that showed that such acts of clumsiness were not an uncommon occurrence in the Capon home.

"How many people are you expecting? There seems to be an awful lot of people here already."

"Well, Miss Smy, I must admit to not counting the invitations. I did have a list and was working at first from that, but then I couldn't find it. I've probably sent it with one of the invitations. Now, Mrs Pilbeam, could you indulge an old man and allow him just two moments of talking cricket with your good husband? Vicar, I take it you've read about Yorkshire's sound thumping of Somerset?"

"Hirst's one hundred and seven seemed to have knocked the stuffing out of them, Colonel. Innings defeat..."

Miss Smy and Mrs Pilbeam had chosen to edge away from the men's conversation and wandered over to the table to inspect the various plates and jugs that had already been deposited onto it by the tireless - if somewhat now damp - Mary.

"Cricket, cricket, cricket," sighed Mrs Pilbeam. "My husband has an uncanny recall of bible verses and cricket minutiae but would struggle to recall what he ate for breakfast. Oh, isn't that Monsieur Gaspard?"

Miss Smy looked up to see Gaspard staring at another area of the large lawn and, following his gaze, rested her own eyes upon the Balthasar family. She looked back at Gaspard and noticed that he was oblivious to all but the small group of people who had caught his eye. Mrs Balthasar looked so beautifully attired that she seemed quite out of place amongst the others in the crowd. However fine the clothes were of those who surrounded her, they were decidedly provincial when compared to Mrs Balthasar's quite superior finery.

But it was not Mrs Balthasar who peeled away from the family group to walk towards Marc-Antoine Gaspard, but Herr Balthasar. Smy detected a small degree of discomfort emerging in the previously self-assured stance of Gaspard as Balthasar neared. The two men stood an awkward distance apart and, to one as intuitive as Winifred Smy, she could detect that the conversation that now passed between them was polite, if a little strained. Balthasar then appeared to be asking Gaspard to join his family but, with his customary charm, the Frenchman seemed to decline the offer.

"He is very good-looking, isn't he? He'll not be alone for very long this afternoon, I'm sure."

It was Mrs Pilbeam who had offered this observation and Smy raised her eyebrows to her in a gentle admonition of the vicar's wife's gossipy relish.

"Oh, Miss Smy, he appears to be coming our way. Time I was off. Ah, Mrs Gooding! Could you spare a moment?" And, with that request of a surprised Mrs Gooding, Mrs Pilbeam absented herself whilst Gaspard bore down on his prey.

"Miss Smy, how delightful. I was hoping that you would be joining us today. Isn't the weather beautiful?"

"You've been in England too long if you use the weather as the opening to your conversations. By the way, when do you return to Paris?"

"Oh, nothing's been decided as yet. I'll stay for perhaps a week or two. Can I get you a drink? A little wine perhaps?"

"That's good of you to offer but I must keep a clear head today."

It was then that Smy noticed a troubled Inspector Tranmer, who had positioned himself on the periphery of the garden and was slowly circling the throng like a watchful sheepdog.

"Tell me, do you know the Balthasars?"

Gaspard took his time to answer, now fully aware that Miss Smy never asked a first question that didn't have a second one closely following it. "Oh, a little. Why do you ask?"

"Why shouldn't I ask? Herr Balthasar certainly seems to know you."

Gaspard sipped his wine, which Smy knew to be a tactic to give himself time to think through his reply.

"Balthasar and I had some business dealings a long time ago. I was astonished to see him here of all places. A marvellous coincidence, don't you think? A Parisian and a Salzburger meeting up here in this wonderful county."

Winifred Smy looked as if she was about to reply to his question, but then seemed to change her mind. Gaspard, sensing that he had failed to convince her with his answer, continued, "He is a very successful man. And a very rich man. But one can forgive him for that."

"I understand that Colonel Capon has arranged a little presentation later. Will you be attending?"

"Of course. If you are attending also it will turn the invitation from an obligation into a pleasure."

"Monsieur Gaspard, it is quite the talent you have being able to communicate your insincerity so convincingly in a second language. Or perhaps you have mastered other tongues equally as well. Yes, I will be there and am looking forward to it."

Rather than be offended by Smy's reply, he bowed his head slightly at her as if she had conferred a great honour on him. "You are too kind, mademoiselle."

"And isn't Herr Balthasar's wife very lovely? She is wearing quite the most stunning dress."

"Hmm? Is she? I didn't notice. As I said, her husband is very rich, so such dresses will be easily affordable for her."

"I detect a little jealousy in your remark."

"Jealousy? Why should I be jealous? I hardly know the woman."

Miss Smy studied Gaspard as she drank her rose lemonade. "So, you do know her then?"

The sound of a horn interrupted them and they both turned to see the Chevalliers' car arriving through the lime trees that lined the long drive that led down to Kenton Hall.

"I think the days of the British nobility's carriage drawing up outside your stately homes are now a thing of the past."

"We seem to be living through a time of great change,

Monsieur Gaspard. One seems to see evidence of it every day. So many people are worried about Europe going to war with itself. What do you think?"

"A war. Of course not. The Kaiser is an ambitious man, but not an uncivilised one. Besides, he knows that if he were to light the fuse, then our two great nations would repel him."

"Herr Balthasar did not seem to share your optimism."

"Herr Balthasar's interests do not extend beyond money. And what he does not already possess, he steals."

32

A SLIGHT THAWING

A light wind now moved amongst and through the crowds, and the high heat of the day was beginning to return to a more comfortable temperature. Gradually, more and more guests were arriving at Kenton Hall and the happy chatter of the adults intermingled with the guileless laughter of the children.

Colonel Capon, always the perfect host, moved steadily through the throng remembering not only the names of all those he met, but even the names of their children and grandchildren as well. He would fix his eyes on someone in such a way that they might feel that they and the Colonel were the only people in an empty room, rather than one of many at a large garden party. The Colonel would then, with a gentle touch on the arm, make the politest excuse and move on to the next of his guests.

Of course, the acute observer might detect that - since his wife's death - such a task was carried out by the Colonel with a slightly more forced air, but he still had the power to charm all who were there.

Miss Smy, feeling in need of refreshing her glass, went to one of the tables and, as she was pouring her rose lemonade, suddenly heard a voice she recognised.

"This is a very lovely gathering."

It was Berthe, who had also come to the table to recharge the glasses of Mr and Mrs Balthasar.

"It certainly is. Can I get something for you, Berthe? The rose lemonade is a particular favourite of mine."

"Thank you but no. If I was not working and also back in Paris, I would enjoy some *pastis*. One sip and I am instantly home again."

"Are you from Marseilles, perhaps?"

"Why, yes! How did you know?"

"Because I once heard you use the phrase, "*Les yeux bordés d'anchois*" when you referred to how tired someone looked, which I associate only with Provence. And it is no secret that *pastis* has a strong connection with Marseilles in particular."

"I am astonished by your knowledge. I only wish that we had got to know each other better when you were working at Grove Hall. Perhaps we might have lunch together when I have my afternoon off?"

"Perhaps. Is Augustus also with you?"

"He is. He told me that he visited you very recently. I do hope that he behaved with some restraint. He can be, if I may say, rather passionate sometimes."

Having filled her glass, Miss Smy placed the jug of lemonade back on the table. "He did come to see me. But I'm struggling to remember why. Does he always share his movements with the staff of the house?"

"He has always confided a little in me, Miss Smy. Perhaps more than he should. I was only a little older than him when

I joined the Balthasar household. We have grown up together, so you might say."

"If I were Augustus' parents, I might take exception to a member of staff expressing such an opinion."

At this, Berthe's face became fixed, resuming the blankness that all servants perfect when in service to their masters and mistresses. "Enjoy the rest of your afternoon, Miss Smy. It has been pleasant to talk with you again."

Winifred Smy reflected on the strange fact that some people are so sure of their ability to manipulate others, that they seriously underestimate the perceptiveness and intelligence of those they are trying to influence. She watched Berthe return to the Balthasars' group, diligently passing the glasses from her tray to Mr and Mrs Balthasar.

What suddenly struck her was how the death of Cavenham was an event that had, to her astonishment, seemed to pass almost unnoticed. Yes, the matter was now resolved as far as the police were concerned - even though their hunt for the perpetrator had so far proved futile - but the murder itself had gone largely unnoticed by the press. When she had asked Manners about it, he wouldn't reply but drew his forefinger across his throat to indicate to her that any mention of it would be career suicide for him. But, she had concluded, this silence wasn't such a difficult thing to achieve for a man of Wenzel Balthasar's wealth.

The sounds of different conversations were carried upon the wind and lost amongst the sound of chattering sparrows and the pattering of the breeze-blown leaves. Inspector Tranmer had abandoned his circumnavigation of the party and was now returning from a neighbouring drinks table with a glass of water in his hand. Catching the eye of Miss Smy, he walked over but was still a little wary of the mood he might find her in.

"Are you still speaking to me?"

"I'm speaking to you now, Inspector, so one would assume so."

"I noticed that the Balthasars are here today. They seem to be getting on with the Chevalliers rather well, don't you think?"

"I think it's not the presence of the Chevalliers that is uppermost in their minds at this moment. I would say there is someone here that they would rather wish elsewhere. Perhaps one of them is wishing them elsewhere more than the others."

Tranmer swirled the ice cube in his glass. "More riddles, Miss Smy. And I suspect you see riddles where none exist. Can I take it that all of your suspicions are now closed? Eary's dead. Cavenham's dead. It's time we all put these terrible happenings in the past."

"I am quite satisfied about the death of Mr Cavenham. But the murder of Thomas Eary is still very much alive to me."

"Then that's for you and you alone to fret about. There isn't a soul here – or in Kenton for that matter – that wants to reopen that scar again."

"Whether people want to reopen the scar or not is of no concern to me. And I can tell you most solemnly, Inspector, even if this does sound like Christ's prediction to Peter, before this day is out, there will be some agitated minds related to Thomas Eary's murder."

"I'm staggered by your arrogance. What right have you to become judge and jury in this matter? If you have any material evidence that is connected with the case, which I must remind you is now firmly closed, then you must communicate that evidence to me."

Smy moved closer to the Inspector but with her back to the

main crowd. "Inspector, I do not consider myself the 'judge and jury' in this matter. From the moment I saw Mr Eary's body I have had only one aim: to discover the truth behind his death. Unlike others I may mention, I could not satisfy myself with easy answers and, the more I turned over the facts that were evident to me, the more committed I became to pursuing the truth. You are right, I now know things that you do not know because, once certain facts had arranged themselves into a neat order for you and your colleagues, you all chose to stop looking."

"Then you must tell me what those facts are. Withholding evidence is a criminal offence."

"That's the second time I've heard you say that to me. Tell me, are you about to arrest me again? Probably not. Let me ask a question of you: do you know the difference between a suffragette and a suffragist?"

Tranmer shook his head. "I take it that they are not the same?"

"Entirely different. At first, I would have called myself a suffragist. My conviction was that if we could put the plain facts in front of those in power, they would immediately move to enhance the position of women so that they could stand equal to men. But I was foolishly naive. Such facts were inconvenient truths to a Government steeped in patriarchy. The facts were merely set aside."

"And a suffragette, Miss Smy?"

"Deeds not words, Inspector. Deeds not words."

33

TRUTH IS NOW SERVED IN THE DINING ROOM

"Ah, Frau Balthasar! Good of you to join us. And your husband?" A few seconds later, Balthasar followed his wife to also enter Kenton Hall's dining room. It was an elegant oak-panelled room with three double-height windows along the south-facing side, divided by long mauve curtains that set off the golden frames of the various family portraits. An overwhelming scent of wood polish hung in the air.

"This is a magnificent dining room table, Colonel."

"Thank you, Herr Balthasar. Burr walnut I was once told but, as with so many other practical matters, I am rather an ignoramus about such things. Ah, Monsieur Gaspard!"

"I apologise for my lateness. I am afraid...ah, we meet again, Herr Balthasar. Good afternoon, Frau Balthasar. I do hope that you are enjoying your return to England."

The Colonel, perceiving that there was an awkwardness about the meeting, decided to take the initiative. "Then we are complete. I believe that you both may not know Monsieur

Gaspard. He has been staying as my guest these past few weeks. Delightful fellow. Knew his father. Of course that was all a very long time ago."

"We are already acquainted, Colonel," said Mrs Balthasar rather coldly. "In Paris, our paths occasionally crossed."

"Did they? Well, by Jove. It *is* a small world, eh?"

"My husband and I were told that there was to be a presentation of some kind. I had expected more people to be here."

"Well, dash it all, I don't know anything about this presentation meself, dear Frau. You see..."

"Please forgive me. The deceit is mine. I needed to see the three of you alone and, knowing that the three of you were guests today, this seemed to be the perfect opportunity." Winifred Smy had entered by another door and now moved around to the head of the long dining room table. "The Colonel was entirely unaware of my intentions, but it was imperative that I saw you today. I have some rather awful news to share."

"Awful news? About what, exactly? My dear Miss Smy, if there was something you wanted to communicate to Herr Balthasar and myself, then you should have made an appointment through the proper channels."

"If I had thought that you would have also welcomed Monsieur Gaspard to such a meeting, then that would have indeed been the action I would have taken. But I suspect that his presence in your home would not have been welcome. Colonel, may I have a private word with your guests?"

Colonel Capon, relieved to be given leave to return to the garden party, hastily did so. Gaspard drew back a chair, sat down and lit a cigarette. "It is good to see you again, Véronique. You look...you look well."

"If you are referring to me, monsieur, then I respectfully

suggest you address me as either Frau or Mrs Balthasar." She then threw a scornful glance at Miss Smy. "I am not sure I want to stay to hear whatever it is that you want to say. You have entirely ruined my afternoon with your antics. Wenzel, I would like to go."

But Herr Balthasar remained unmoved. The small twitches just discernible in his face seemed triggered by a series of unsettling thoughts. "My dear, I think I would like to listen to whatever it is that Miss Smy wants to communicate. I suspect that most of it will already be known to us."

"You are right, Herr Balthasar. Much of what I want to relate is known to you. In fact, the three of you may well correct me on some points. But I also have intelligence that you - I am sure - do not know. You may think that my arranging this meeting is an impertinence but, by the time we all leave this room, I am certain that you will have agreed that it was the only course of action I could have taken."

Gaspard, who was by the minute growing more and more exasperated, exclaimed, "Please, if you have something to tell us, then tell us! This whole charade of yours has already pushed my patience quite beyond its limits!"

Miss Smy held the back of the chair that she was standing behind and drew it towards her as if it were the final line of defence that she might have to call on as the next hour unfolded. After taking a short breath, she turned to Gaspard. "I think your choice of the word charade is the *mot juste*. Ever since we met that first time in the churchyard, you have been careful to appear as someone entirely different. You are no more a music critic for *Le Petit Parisien* than I am. It was a flimsy disguise which you believed that no one would be able to see through. In fact, so confident were you in your charade that you didn't even disguise your name. After all, who in Suffolk - as uneducated as you no doubt find us - would ever have heard of Marc-Antoine Gaspard, the artist."

Véronique Balthasar looked incredulously at Gaspard. "Music critic? You? Whatever made you want to tell people that?"

But Gaspard chose not to reply, and sank a little lower into his chair, studying the orange glow of his cigarette. "It was just a game. Sometimes it's nice to be somebody else."

"And you were right to see through my deliberate mistake about the true composer of *The Rite of Spring*. But to be a music critic and not attend a ballet that was already rumoured to be quite sensational convinced me that you were lying to me. But I think it was your conversation about Debussy in my kitchen that convinced me of your, shall I say, act. You looked at a picture on my wall and instantly offered an artistic critique. You then espied a score by Debussy and could only remark on the marital shortcomings of the man, and not a mention of his undoubted genius as a composer. However, by that time I had asked a colleague if he could establish your true identity and, in a few days, he gave me details - verified by a Parisian newspaper contact - of who you really were."

"You are too harsh, Mademoiselle. All I wanted was to spend some time away and to stop being the 'well-known artist'. Besides, is music so far removed from art?"

"Are you really a well-known artist? You have received very little critical acclaim in your career and yet claim that you needed to travel under some false professional guise but still chose to retain your real name."

"I know exactly why he did not want to change his name," broke in Wenzel Balthasar. "He knew that, sooner or later, my wife would hear of his presence in the area. I'm afraid that that has been a recurring pattern over the recent years. It was being hounded by this man that eventually drove her to leave France and return to Suffolk."

"But you have always had Monsieur Gaspard present in your house, wherever you have moved to, Herr Balthasar."

"What are you talking about? Are you saying that this man is often in my house? Unless I have been cruelly deceived, this man has been a stranger to my home."

"What Miss Smy is leading up to is Gaspard's paintings, Wenzel. Isn't that so, Miss Smy? You knew about the paintings."

"I am not sure that the subject is entirely relevant to what I want to tell you but, yes, there are several of Gaspard's canvases about your house, but mostly in the first room we met in for my interview. What initially intrigued me was that, when one looked closely at certain paintings, there was no artist's signature. I soon noticed that all of the unsigned pictures were obviously executed by the same painter. I then took the trouble to carefully study each picture, and one thing soon became apparent: it was not that the paintings had not been signed, but that the signature on each canvas had been skilfully painted out."

"Painted out? Who would paint the signature out?"

"I'm afraid it was me, Wenzel. I am not going to lie to you." Mrs Balthasar suddenly looked weary and reached for a chair.

"But you gave me an assurance that your involvement with this...with this so-called artist was over years ago!"

"And it is! But what else could I do? After all, he...I have already said too much."

"Mrs Balthasar, you were about to say what everyone in this room already knows, including me. Monsieur Gaspard is Melka's father."

34

MRS BALTHASAR'S INTERESTING CONDITION

The room was silent. Small drifts of smoke from Gaspard's cigarette pirouetted in slow spirals towards the ceiling.

"I did say that some of what I wanted to relate was already known."

"First, I am intrigued as to how you found out this information. And second, I fail to understand why you should think that bringing us into this room to tell us what we already know might have some merit."

"Herr Balthasar, these facts related to Melka are not my primary source of interest. But they do have some bearing on those matters that you do not know about."

"But can I remind you of my first question? How did you arrive at what you now think you know?"

"My first suspicion was aroused by two people who were present at Melka's christening. When I first told them that I was working with Melka who was now in the safekeeping of her godmother, they were surprised. Their recall of Melka's

187

christening was that it was not Mrs Balthasar who was the godmother but someone else quite different. When I visited the woman who was purportedly Melka's mother, Mrs Eary that is, I established something rather intriguing when I asked if I could see her ears."

"Her ears?" repeated Herr Balthasar.

"Oh, yes. When I first sat with Melka, I immediately noticed that her earlobes were attached to the side of her head. This is rather rare; most people's earlobes are unattached, as both yours, mine and Monsieur Gaspard's are. According to a very good medical friend of mine, such earlobes can be a genetic inheritance, but she also pointed out that this is not foolproof. Parents with free earlobes have been known to have a child with attached earlobes."

Mrs Balthasar stood up and drew the locks of her hair back from the side of her face. "Exhibit one, if you please. I have attached earlobes as well. What Miss Smy is trying to tell you with her nauseating circumlocution is that this information would imply that I am Melka's mother. Is that not so, Miss Smy?"

"Do you deny it?" responded Winifred Smy. "We four have already established who the father is. Now I think we can agree on who Melka's mother is as well."

Mrs Balthasar resumed her seat but this time there was a defiant expression on her face. "I am not sure I wish to continue this conversation. Who the devil do you think you are to stand there with your righteous manner passing judgment over us all? I think we've all heard enough."

"Hear, hear," added Gaspard. "This fascinating dissection of our lives has ruined my appetite alarmingly. Perhaps, with your permission, of course, Miss Smy, we might be permitted to go now?"

"I am not compelling you to stay, Monsieur Gaspard. After all, your heartless treatment of Véronique Goymer would not make for pleasant listening. I was rather surprised, when you were in my house, that you should be so dismissive of the behaviour of Claude Debussy to his first wife, and yet had failed to mention that there was a time when your behaviour towards a woman who was carrying your child was equally chilling."

Gaspard now stood up with a fierce anger. "How dare you! How dare you say such things. You were not there! You could not know!"

"But she does know, doesn't she? We all know, Marc-Antoine, how you deserted my wife when she was with child. Your child."

Gaspard stomped off towards the far window. His face alive with an intense fury.

Miss Smy raised her voice a little so that Gaspard could hear her at the far end of the dining room. "I would like to tell the three of you what I know. I would also like you to tell me if what I know is wrong. Mrs Balthasar, Some time ago I spoke with a Mr Bridges, Bunny Bridges, as he is better known. He once worked at Nacton Racecourse, just outside Ipswich, and knew your father well. He recalled that an Arthur Goymer was invited to work at Chantilly, a very superior racing course outside Paris. Apparently, whilst he was working there, he met a French woman and they had a daughter, whom they christened Véronique. When Véronique was of school age, she was sent to Ipswich Grammar School, to finish her education."

"Miss Smy, this is tedious. Once again, you are just telling us everything we already know."

"True, Mrs Balthasar, but please be assured that it is most

germane to what I eventually have to tell you. You see, although you boarded at Ipswich school during term time, you went and stayed with your father's sister and her husband, Thomas Eary. I think I am correct in that?"

Mrs Balthasar looked away.

"And, if I may continue, you stayed with the Earys until you were sixteen years of age or so. Then you returned to France, blessed with one outstanding skill - you were a painter of no mean talent. Your father's patron, the Duc D'Aumale, had great influence and, just before the turn of the last century, you were one of the first women to enrol at the *École des Beaux-Arts*. I believe it was whilst you were there that you first met Marc-Antoine Gaspard, a fellow pupil?"

"Why ask? You appear to know everything about me. But I still fail to see where all this is leading."

"Oh, that will become very apparent, believe me. You and Monsieur Gaspard became very close and, in 1901, you discovered yourself to be in the family way, if you will permit me to use an expression of my mother's. My sources tell me that it was at that moment that Melka's father chose to absent himself from your life."

Smy looked towards Gaspard, who was continuing to stare out of the window at the happy crowd assembled on the lawns outside. His shoulders dropped a little and his chin sank to his chest. "I was so young. I was in such a state of panic! Believe me, Miss Smy. I loved Véronique so much but was overwhelmed by the news. Yes, you are right, I ran away. I was - in fact, I still am - a coward. I was also, and still am, in love with Véronique."

"And then you, Herr Balthasar, entered into the drama of these young lives, a respectable widower with a young son, Augustus. You were already a close hunting friend of the Duc

D'Aumale, and had yourself fallen for Véronique Goymer. How you came to know of her plight I do not know, but I do know that you arranged the passage of her newborn child to the Earys to save the reputation of the woman who had agreed to be your wife. You even arranged and attended Melka's christening to make sure that it went smoothly."

"It was important to me that I could reassure Véronique that the child was being cared for. But tell me, how did you know I was there? I tried to make myself invisible as much as I could."

"A small slip of concentration on your part. One person who was there thought they heard you say the word 'bitter' when you handed the card bearing the name you wanted the child to be called. Of course, in your own language, you were saying the word 'please'."

"It was so long ago that I don't remember even saying that. But you are right. Véronique and I had settled on the name Melka and that was what was on the card that I handed to the priest."

"And you, Mrs Balthasar, I do not know the agonies that you must have gone through over the years, not being able to be there to watch your own daughter grow. I also do not know the moment that you decided that you wanted to be near her again, but that is what you did. You persuaded your husband to move to Suffolk with the sole intention of reclaiming not only the affection of your daughter, but the rightful ownership as well."

"And how naive I was. Mrs Eary would often write to tell me about how Melka was progressing, but the letters only told me so much. Eventually, it wasn't enough and I wanted to be the mother I had never been for her. I wanted to give her a better life, the life I had enjoyed when I was in France. The life that Wenzel and I had the power to create for her."

Gaspard turned on Mrs Balthasar. "But that was so selfish of you! How ever could you think that you could just tear a child away from the only life she had known and expect her to suddenly turn her affection from the Earys to you? What were you thinking of? Has your money deprived you of your senses? Of your humanity?"

"At least I wanted to do something for her! You...you just deserted her! Abandoned her! What right do you think you have telling me where I may have failed her. You failed her before she was even born!"

"Please, please, please *schatzi*. This isn't helping. It's not helping you or Melka. Miss Smy, we have found out in this room that the effects of our best intentions have caused much pain. But that is a matter for us three to resolve between us. With great respect, I do believe that this distressing conversation could have taken place without your involvement. Perhaps we might all agree to close this meeting now and rejoin the Colonel's garden party?"

Miss Smy held up her hands to indicate that no one should leave. "No, I cannot let you do that. What we have spoken about up to this point has been significant for another reason."

"What other reason?" asked Gaspard.

"The reason why Mr Thomas Eary was murdered, and the part that each of you played in that murder."

35

THE GLINT OF THE SUN

"What are you talking about, woman? What do you mean by the part *we* played in his murder? It wasn't murder, it was an accident. The police themselves said so. Isn't that true, Wenzel?"

"I can assure you, Mrs Balthasar, it was no accident. Of course, some people would like us to think so, but I am utterly convinced that Thomas Eary was murdered."

Gaspard snorted derisively at Miss Smy's assertion. "Murdered? My dear mademoiselle, it was no such thing."

Mrs Balthasar found herself suddenly in agreement with Gaspard. "I second that! You're allowing your imagination to run away with you. It's a preposterous notion."

"Have you never asked yourself, Mrs Balthasar, what Mr Eary was doing in a wood that bordered the grounds of your residence?"

"He was poaching. That's what I was told. You know as well as I do that Suffolk is overrun with them. I sometimes think we have more poachers than rabbits in this county."

Miss Smy smiled patiently, "Mr Eary lives in Clopton, which

is some eight miles or so from Grove Hall. According to one, how should I put it...authority on such matters, there are many areas of land which would be far more attractive to any poacher wishing to put a rabbit in his pot. There are other facts as well that you would be wise to consider. Mr Thomas Eary was to many who knew him, a fine man of some great integrity. Surely that is the man you remember when you were young? And isn't that the very reason why you entrusted your precious newborn child into his care?"

"People can change," said Mrs Balthasar petulantly.

"No, Mr Eary was as Mr Eary always was. But then he and his wife became an inconvenience to you, didn't they? You wanted Melka back and Thomas Eary wanted her to stay where she was. All of a sudden, the Earys had changed from a convenience into an impediment."

"Are you suggesting..."

"No, Mrs Balthasar, merely observing. We all know in this room that he wasn't in that wood because he was poaching. He was in that wood on that day so that he could watch someone he had grown to love. He couldn't let her go. At one time in his life, he was asked to return his much-loved Véronique to her parents in Chantilly. Asking him to now allow his precious Melka to return to someone else's care was one step too far. Remember this was the man who had been asked to play the role of her father."

"But why was he carrying a gun? Wenzel, you said you saw the gun that they found in the wood where he'd been hiding."

"No, my dear. I said I was told that he was carrying a gun. I didn't actually see a gun."

"And did you see a gun, Monsieur Gaspard?"

"Me? Why would I see a gun? I wasn't even there."

"But you were there, weren't you, Mr Gaspard? My best guess, and I do stress that it is my best guess, is that, when you first arrived at Kenton Hall, you wanted it made known to the neighbourhood that you were staying with Colonel Capon. Why? Because, as Herr Balthasar has already stated, you wanted Mrs Balthasar to realise that you had also come to Suffolk with, I am sure, the sole intention of making her acquaintance once again. That is why we first met in the church that day. You wanted to be seen in the parish, and carefully contrived to place yourself in any situation where, perhaps, yours and Mrs Balthasar's paths would cross. You became a rather regular attendee at All Saints Church, for example, always seated at the back where you could watch who entered during the service."

"Ridiculous! I am a sociable man. Is one not allowed to transfer one's dilettante habits from the town to the countryside?"

Miss Smy moved around the table towards Gaspard, who was still standing at the high window. "It was rather underhand of me, I know, but I asked one of the servants at Kenton Hall where you were on the day that Eary died. They told me that you had gone for a long walk and had informed them that you would not return to Kenton Hall in time for lunch. Can I suggest that you - like Thomas Eary - also made for the wood behind Grove Hall? I think you had the intention not only of catching a glimpse of your daughter - but her mother as well. I imagine you placed your stick down, sat with your back to a tree and drank copiously from your cognac flask."

"And you have some proof of this, Miss Smy?"

Winifred Smy reached into her pocket and held up the lid to Gaspard's flask.

"You found that in the wood?"

"In the wood, Monsieur. But you also lost one other prized

possession."

Gaspard returned to his seat and sighed heavily. "You are about to tell me I also lost my beautiful walking stick. You can save your breath. I did lose my walking stick. But it was not in the state you found it. I heard someone coming through the trees. I thought it might be a bailiff. What with all the cognac, and it being a hot day and everything, I panicked and couldn't see where I had left my stick. I must have thought that it was better to come back for it later, and so crept away."

"I believe you. You see, I would hazard that the person you heard coming was Thomas Eary. I don't think he had seen you or, if he had, he'd made sure that you were gone before taking up a position himself where he could see his beloved Melka. Perhaps he wanted to make some sort of communication with her. If so, my presence on the lawn with her that day would have discouraged him."

"And it was whilst he was concentrating on what Melka was doing that he must have stumbled and shot himself. Surely that's what happened, Miss Smy?"

"I think not, Herr Balthasar. You see, it is only at a distance that one can sometimes reassemble events and perceive those hidden truths that eluded one at first. For example, why had Mr Eary already sustained a heavy blow to the side of his neck? It was quite apparent to the Doctor who examined him, but curiously set aside when the police were considering the possible train of events. I propose that it was caused by a blow from a heavy piece of wood. Perhaps a thick branch or..." and Miss Smy turned to Gaspard as she paused, "A walking stick."

"I thought you said you believed me?"

"Oh, I do believe you. It is a bizarre justification on my part, I know, but your love of that walking stick is so apparent that it would be impossible for me to accept that you would use it in such a violent way. But in the short time that you had left and Mr Eary had taken up his position, I believe a third – and possibly a fourth person – was already making their way to the rear of the garden. Why? Because I believe they had detected a suspicious presence on the edge of that wood. I am certain that a glint from your flask betrayed your position, Monsieur Gaspard, to someone who was looking out from Grove Hall. The morning I first met you, you pulled that same flask out and drank from it. It was immediately noticeable to me then how easily it glinted and caught the sun on that morning."

Wenzel Balthasar now interrupted Smy. "But why do you think the person who saw the light from the flask would have been in Grove Hall? They could have been anywhere."

"Oh, that's easy. At the time, Melka and I were the only people in the grounds on that side of the house. The gardeners had retired for a break, so the only possible explanation must be that it would have been someone looking out from the Hall."

Now Gaspard cut in. "I need to be clear on this, Miss Smy. You're telling me that I alerted someone to my presence with my flask but, by the time I had left and this poor man Eary had taken my place, yet another person had arrived at the scene?"

"Yes. I am of the mind that the glint from your flask alerted someone who was in the house. Perhaps they thought a trespasser or poacher was lurking at the edge of the wood. But they immediately responded by stealthily walking around the outside of the grounds – remaining out of sight as they did so – and, upon finding a man spying on someone out on the lawn, chanced upon the stick that Monsieur Gaspard had failed to find and hit the man hard on the side of the neck. May I read something to you?"

Once again, Miss Smy reached into the pocket of her skirt and pulled out a piece of paper, which revealed itself to be a letter.

"I have a great friend in Aldeburgh of some considerable medical distinction. It was her that helped me understand the possible inheritance of Melka's earlobes. She will be someone that Herr and Mrs Balthasar will get to know in time. I wrote to her about the bruising and my theory that an ebony walking stick may well have been its cause. She was good enough to write back, *"A quick blow to the carotid artery on the side of the neck may well render a person unconscious. In some cases, I have known it to cause death due to a sudden drop in blood pressure in the brain. At the very least, a strike on the wind pipe will have its victim gasping for air."*

"So that's what happened to my beautiful stick. It is...it is an uncivilised act to cause such damage to..."

"To a human being, Monsieur Gaspard? For that is what it did. And yet, for our murderer, the violence was not yet complete. For as Mr Eary stumbled from the thicket that he was hiding behind, the murderer shot him in cold blood. He ran pathetically forward onto the lawn and died almost instantly."

There was an appalled stillness in the room. The sounds of laughter and raised voices could just be heard from the garden and were in stark contrast to the sombre mood that was deepening in the dining room.

"You're reading too much into this. This is all just overheated supposition. Why ever do you think that someone in our very own house..."

"Mrs Balthasar, I have yet to point to those facts that transmute this supposition into hard evidence. Allow me to take you back to that dreadful day. You see, at first, I couldn't remember if the gunshot I had heard rang out before I saw Mr Eary emerge from the bushes, or afterwards. But then I remembered that having been immediately alerted by the sound of a gun, I turned to see Mr Eary already stumbling across the lawn. He was some yards away from the edge of the wood, so he must have been shot whilst clear of the undergrowth. That decided the first fact for me that he had not shot himself but been shot by another person."

"There is a second fact, Miss Smy?" coolly asked Herr Balthasar.

"Indeed there is one which instantly struck me. When I turned over the body of Thomas Eary, I realised that he couldn't have shot himself."

Wenzel Balthasar, who had been standing for the entire conversation up to this point, now chose to sit down. "So enlighten us, Miss Smy." The tone of his voice had become weary and resigned. Miss Smy half-smiled at this change in his manner.

"Forgive me if what I am about to say is upsetting to any of you. There are three factors present when a person is shot: the proximity of the assailant, the weapon's calibre and the type of ammunition being used. All combine to produce a pattern to a gunshot wound. The entrance wound of a bullet is normally smaller and neater, whereas the exit wound can often be less symmetrical and feature bone and muscle damage, or torn areas of tissue and skin. What was instantly apparent was the discolouration of Mr Eary's skin where it had been burnt by the gunpowder. These facts clearly indicated to me that he had been shot from behind, something which is next to impossible if one shoots oneself. The fact is that self-inflicted wounds that prove rapidly fatal are either to the front of the body or to the head."

"You are quite certain of this? Why have you spotted something that has not been discovered by the police?"

"Because, Herr Balthasar, when one has firmly made up one's mind about something, one ceases to search for facts that contradict one's conclusion. We all do it, so why should we take the moral high ground when the local constabulary shares the same weakness? Tell an overworked doctor to quickly confirm an obvious accident and, being human as they are, that is what they will do. An independent assessment is even more unlikely when the doctor who often assists in post-mortems in this area of Suffolk has a fondness for alcohol at any time of the day or night."

Mrs Balthasar calmly rose from her seat. "I think I've heard more than enough for one day. Wenzel, will you call for our carriage?"

"My dear, I know this is exceedingly wearing for you, but I must ask one thing of Miss Smy and then we will go home."

Mrs Balthasar looked annoyed and slumped back into her seat.

"Miss Smy, you have brought us this far. You say you know who murdered Mr Eary. I must know who that person is before I leave this room."

Miss Smy walked over to the corner of the dining room and reached for a scroll of drawing paper which she then held up. "This picture, which Melka was drawing just before Mr Eary died, has the answer to your question, Herr Balthasar."

36

AN OPEN WINDOW

There was a sharp knock on the dining room door. "Come in," said Véronique Balthasar.

Tilly Carter, one of Colonel Capon's housemaids, entered with a tray. "Master thought that you might find some tea refreshing. Shall I leave it here for you?"

"Yes, please do. Thank you."

"Thank you, Ma'am." Tilly glanced quickly at Gaspard who winked mischievously at her as she left.

Miss Smy waited until the door was closed before opening out Melka's drawing. "Herr Balthasar, would you be so good as to pass me two teacups?" She took the cups from him and placed one at each side of the picture, to prevent it from rolling up again.

"As you will see, Melka has inherited the artistic gifts of her parents. Her mastery of drawing is utterly exceptional and, I must say, the detail in this picture quite astonishes me."

Gaspard was first to the front of the room and surveyed his daughter's work with a satisfied smile on his face. "This is a very fine drawing. Compositionally a little stilted but her rendering of the shadows and textures is excellent."

"Mrs Balthasar, would you care to see it?"

Mrs Balthasar remained in her seat. "I have already seen it, Miss Smy. I cannot look at it without thinking about what happened on the day she executed it. But I am still at a loss as to its relevance to these discussions."

"If you look closely at the detail of the house, you will see that all of the upper windows are closed. After all, it was a very hot afternoon and one of your servants, Selina, told me that she always closes the curtains during the day to keep all of the rooms cool. But, if you look closely at each of the bedroom windows that Melka has drawn, there is one that is definitely open."

"That looks like..."

"Exactly, Herr Balthasar. It is Augustus' bedroom window. My theory is that only he could have seen that there was movement at the back of the garden. According to Selina, he refused her entry into his bedroom that afternoon because he claimed to be ill. Selina was certain that there was someone in the room with him, but discreetly kept that fact to herself until I questioned her, as she was worried that if she revealed who it was, then she might lose her job. I think that having espied an interloper hiding at the back of the garden, Augustus thought it his duty to deal with him and crept around the side of the garden until he was in sight of Thomas Eary. I am certain that he then spotted Monsieur Gaspard's walking stick and used it as a cudgel to render him unconscious."

"This is preposterous, Miss Smy! You are accusing my son of involvement in this man's murder based on a drawing! Have you quite lost your senses?"

"I did not accuse him of murder, Herr Balthasar. Assault, yes;

murder, no. I have brought you this far, please let me beg your continuing patience. You see, I think that there was another person present at the time. Let me tell you why. When Mr Eary had been shot and lay in Melka's arms, we were soon joined by several others. The gardeners were first to arrive as they had been enjoying their break. Immediately, one of them ran to the house to alert you all. Herr Balthasar, you were quickly on the scene of the killing, followed by your wife."

"That is right. We had just returned from Ipswich. My wife had some books to collect from her usual bookshop in Dial Lane. I had hardly taken my hat off in the hall when young Matthew told us the news."

You'll also remember that Cavenham arrived with your son not long afterwards?"

"Cavenham! Was it Cavenham who shot him?"

"Let me continue, please, Mrs Balthasar. As people arrived, I took a step back - there was little that I could do - and the group gathering around the dead Mr Eary was soon joined by one more person. It was then that I noticed something rather odd. This last person to join us, and your son, were both carrying the seeds of this plant on the lower parts of their clothes." Winifred Smy held up a long, straggly plant that she had been keeping on the chair beside her. "*Galium aparine* as the Reverend Pilbeam would have it. Or cleavers, as it is more widely known. Why, as your son and this other person told the police in their evidence, did they claim not to have left the house at all that day, when it was obvious that they had. If you look at the place where Mr Eary had been hiding, you will see cleavers everywhere and the seeds are notorious for adhering themselves to the clothes of humans or the fur of animals. Eary's trousers bore many of the seeds, as well as the other two people I have referred to."

"I'm still very sceptical of your theories, Miss Smy. But at least enlighten me as to who this other person was."

"I'm surprised you have not already guessed, Frau Balthasar. Have you not, in your service, one who is utterly devoted to you? One who was very young herself when she became part of your retinue when you first returned to France and has been utterly loyal from that day to this? Someone who, perhaps unbeknown to you but known to all that work for you, has exercised a manipulative hold over Augustus. The rumour amongst the household is that he is completely in thrall to her and the relationship between them is, I would venture, a most unedifying one."

"You do me a dishonour, Miss Smy. I have been well aware that something was going on between Augustus and Berthe. I think you will recall a recent conversation about this very matter, Wenzel? You were rather dismissive of my observation, I'm afraid."

But Wenzel Balthasar's mind was now dizzy with all of the unseemly revelations. "But how do you know that Berthe shot Eary? Their roles might have been reversed."

"Again, things fall into place so neatly with hindsight. In the days that followed did you not notice how often Berthe was troubled by considerable pain in her shoulder? The answer is plain to me: she used the same gun you were carrying when I saw you recently, the day I visited Grove Hall with Inspector Tranmer."

"How can you tell it was my gun?"

"If I am not mistaken, the gun you were carrying that day was a Holland and Holland sidelock double rifle?"

"You impress me, Miss Smy. It was indeed."

"I am aware that such a gun is very expensive, not least

because it would have been manufactured for you to a very personal specification, the width of your shoulders, the length of your arms and so on?"

Holding his hands in the air, he agreed saying, "They even measured the size of these."

"When that same gun is held by another person, in this case, a more petite person, you and I know that such a weapon can be a very different beast. I would propose that the reason that Berthe was in such pain from that day onwards was because of the fierce recoil of the gun. She was standing so close she couldn't have missed Mr Eary - hence the smudge of gunpowder around the wound - but her shoulder would have been forced to accommodate the tremendous kick of the gun as she fired it."

"But what about the gun that was found in the wood?" asked Gaspard.

"That was yet another fact that convinced me that it was murder. I said earlier that, once everyone began to assemble around Mr Eary, I stepped back and walked over to the place from where he had emerged. My first suspicion was that it must have been an accident. At the time, I could find no other explanation. So I inspected the area and I can tell you all here and now, there was no gun to be seen anywhere."

"But the police found his gun! They have it at the station. They told me so."

"No, Herr Balthasar. They found a gun, not *the* gun. You possess an extensive collection of firearms, Sir. But with your superb hunting weapon you probably never even think of taking any other gun when you are intending to shoot. I would propose, later today, that you inspect each of your gun racks when you return. I am confident you will find a weapon missing."

"Oh God! Oh dear God..."

"What is it, Wenzel?"

Balthasar buried his face in his hands. "Miss Smy is right. I had already noticed one of my guns was missing and asked Cavenham about it. He thought that Augustus may have used it and forgotten to return it. I noticed it was still missing only yesterday."

Gaspard, who was now holding Melka's drawing, turned to Miss Smy. "Well, you have mercilessly exposed all of our lives in one way or another, mademoiselle. What do you intend to do now?"

"My intention now is to leave this room and ask Inspector Tranmer to listen to everything I have told you today."

"What if he refuses to listen to you? After all, haven't all enquiries been closed."

Miss Smy did not reply initially but calmly picked up her hat and the wilted sprig of cleavers from the table. "If the Inspector does not want to hear my theory then I know someone who will be very interested in pursuing all of what I have shared with you. From what he told me some time ago, it would offer him the perfect opportunity to repair a rather broken relationship with his editor."

37

THE WALK ALONG CRAG PATH

From where the two women stood beside the Coastguard Lookout Tower, one could see the sea's sluggish waves falling limply onto the shingle as if all energy had been sucked out of the ocean by the heat of the sun. One thin sleeve of cloud stood clear against the deep blue of the sky as gulls flew in effortless glides from one roof ledge to another. Two fishermen, having just hauled their boat onto the shore, leered at the women as they spread out their nets to dry.

"I hear that you've vacated Grove Hall. I'm sure that it has a lot of unhappy memories for you."

"Mrs Chevallier was very kind and suggested that we stay with them at Aspall Hall. I must admit I was glad to do so. We both couldn't bear to stay any longer at Grove Hall and now we have time to find somewhere else."

"Will you stay in Suffolk?"

"We have to now. The police still haven't finished their enquiries and made it clear that they will need to interview Augustus again."

"I was surprised when you told me that he admitted to being

involved in Eary's murder."

Mrs Balthasar allowed herself a rueful smile. "Wenzel is a man of honour and, when he feels that it is being compromised in any way, he becomes...how shall I put this? Persuasive, yes, that's the word. He becomes very persuasive. Between you and I, Miss Smy, I have never cared for Augustus much, but I care for his father a great deal."

"Monsieur Gaspard still appears to hold a great affection for you."

"Do you think so? I'm afraid I loathe the man. You were right. I first met him at the *École des Beaux-Arts*. I was rather naive and fell in love not with Gaspard, but with some silly adolescent notion of falling in love. When I found out that I was with child, I soon woke up to the fact that the idea of spending the rest of my life with him was a most awful prospect. Wenzel may not have Gaspard's charms, but he has other qualities that mean everything to me."

"Can I ask you one thing? Just to satisfy my own curiosity."

"You're going to ask me about Gaspard's paintings, aren't you?"

"Of course, you don't have to answer."

"There's nothing unseemly about the reason why I have his canvases. He was a man constantly in debt and I couldn't stand by and not help. After all, he was still Melka's father and I did it solely for her. It wasn't because of Wenzel that I painted over Gaspard's signature, I'm afraid my husband has no interest whatsoever in art and would never have even looked at them. No, it was because I feared that Augustus might notice and...well, we can both imagine how Augustus might exploit my past."

"Yes, Herr Balthasar does have a rather difficult son. He

certainly doesn't seem to act with the same integrity as your husband."

"I tolerate Augustus' behaviour for Wenzel's sake but have never trusted him. Strangely enough, when it comes to criminal acts, you may be surprised to learn that my stepson is not a very good liar. The moment that Wenzel put your evidence before him, he looked increasingly guilty the more he denied it."

"Yes, I witnessed that for myself. It was just before Colonel Capon's garden party. Augustus came to my house and tried to direct my attention to the fact that guilt for Mr Eary's death lay with...shall we just say another quarter? As you say, he is a rather unconvincing liar. Looking back now, I suspect that Berthe encouraged him to do it. She knew that I had her in my sights the moment I started to ask about her shoulder. By the way, what has become of Berthe?"

"We don't know. Somehow she seemed to have got wind of events and disappeared. They have issued her personal details to all of the country's ports, but Berthe is a very resourceful woman. She is a strange one in many ways. All the years she worked for me, I could never fault her. But there was always something about her that made me feel uneasy. Wenzel told me I was just imagining things, but a woman's intuition..."

"Berthe was completely devoted to you. That much was obvious to me during the short time I worked at Grove Hall. It seemed as if your needs and desires automatically became her needs and desires. You wanted Melka to return to you, and so then did she. When Thomas Eary started to show a reluctance to let Melka go, she cruelly dealt with him on your behalf. I knew there was something unstable about her. That was why I made my request of you and Herr Balthasar that day. An ice-cool murderess such as Berthe is not, shall we say, preferred company for a young girl."

"Quite. Well, Aldeburgh seems safe enough to me."

"By the way, what has Augustus told the police?"

"Apparently he did admit to taking Wenzel's rifle, but only to show off to Berthe how grown up he was. He then said that, when he crept up behind Eary, he spotted a walking stick in the nettles, picked it up and struck him with it which caused Eary to fall, unable to breathe. That was the point, he claims, that Berthe took over and grabbed the rifle from him and, as Eary stumbled out onto the lawn trying to escape, she shot him."

Smy removed her hat and dusted off some sand which had caught in the band of the crown. "And do you believe him?"

"I think I do, but what chills me to the marrow is the composure that both he and Berthe showed, not only just after the killing but the days that followed as well."

"Yes, they certainly had the presence of mind to leave another gun in the bushes where Eary had secreted himself, knowing that that would support the idea that it was all a terrible accident."

"I truly have no idea what will become of Augustus. Wenzel has insisted that, if and when he is released, he should immediately enlist in the Austrian army."

"Ah, the army. It can be the making of some, I hear..." Miss Smy suddenly turned away.

"Are you all right?"

Smy had reached for a handkerchief and was dabbing her eyes. "Of course! Just some sand, I think. I'm all right now. Shall we walk on a little?"

The path ran beside the beach, upon which were many fishing smacks which had been abandoned for the day, their catches already making their way towards the restaurants and markets of various towns and cities. Holidaymakers, dressed down for their week away, ambled along with relaxed smiles, enjoying aimless conversations as they glanced occasionally out at the North Sea.

"You know, Mrs Balthasar, I truly am sorry for all that has happened to your family. I have many faults, I'm afraid, one of which is a tendency to focus obsessively when I feel that a great wrong has been perpetrated. What made it so much worse for me was that Melka was somehow at the centre of it and I feared for her welfare. Looking back now, I realise that I shouldn't have worried. Whatever happened, you and Herr Balthasar would have protected her, but that worry became my primary motivation in seeing justice done."

"You did what you did; I don't blame you for anything. I came to Suffolk with a muddle-headed notion of getting my daughter back and somehow thought that, in this area of Suffolk at least, my history would not be known. Of course, we leave traces of ourselves wherever we go. It wouldn't have been long before another person would have started to ask some awkward questions."

"Yes, that's true. Gossip is a speedy traveller, although so much gets added and lost upon its journey."

"You know, Miss Smy, I really did believe that Mr Eary had accidentally shot himself. I believed it because that was what I wanted everyone to believe. But it was so obvious that he couldn't have."

"You were not the only one to think it. Many were perfectly willing to let the case rest on that conclusion. Apparently, Mr Eary had secreted himself close to your house before. He obviously missed Melka a great deal and loved her very much."

"He was always a good man. When I was young he was so very

caring. Mrs Eary was somewhat different. One received very little affection from her, it was as if she had a limited amount of love and that was reserved only for her husband. But I deeply regret how I sidelined my thoughts and memories of Mr Eary."

"I think he'd already lost you and then couldn't bear to lose a cherished relationship again."

Mrs Balthasar looked at Miss Smy and asked if they may stop walking for a while so that she could gather her thoughts. "You know, I've never been to Aldeburgh before. Somehow it was always a little too far away from Clopton. Tell me, what's Mrs Garrett-Anderson like? She sounds a little formidable to me."

"She is, but then so are you. She is a good woman and has cared for Melka a great deal since she came here." Miss Smy suddenly laughed. "It was Mrs Garrett-Anderson who explained everything to me about inheritance and earlobes. She is a fascinating woman. I met her through Millicent Fawcett, her sister."

"The suffrage campaigner? Were you a suffragette, Miss Smy? If you were, I'd like to hear all about it."

"Some other time, perhaps. It really isn't that...ah, there they are."

At the end of Crag Path came two figures walking towards them. One who was late middle-aged, somewhat stout and stern looking; the other, a small girl.

"Oh, Miss Smy, there's Melka. All of a sudden I'm rather afraid. What should I say? What do I say, Miss Smy?"

"You will find the words in time. For now, take it slowly and replace the anger in your heart with love. I kept a promise this morning and walked by the sea with Melka. I think she wants to rebuild her relationship with you and you will find her a very different little girl to the one you last saw in Grove Hall. Now it is best that I leave you. Goodbye, Frau Balthasar."

Winifred Smy walked through the alley that connected Crag Path with the High Street. Already, the strong odour of ozone had dissipated and the smell of vegetables and the open door of a fishmonger assaulted the senses. A young man was walking ahead of her and, from a door that led into a butcher's shop, emerged a young woman who awkwardly pressed something into his hand. The man, who appeared to blush with what he clearly thought was a romantic encounter, watched the woman as she quickly disappeared into the busy crowd. He then remembered the gift that she had given him and, opening his hand out, looked down to see what it was.

It was a feather. A white feather.

Acknowledgements

Many people have generously contributed their help with this book. First, for her advice and suggestions, unfailing encouragement and tireless patience and support, I would like to thank my wife, Penny. I would also like to extend my appreciation to Maud Henry and Otto Kyrieleis for their correcting of my woeful French and German. The fabulous cover design is, once again, provided by Lucy Johnson and the beautiful artwork used for the front cover is the work of the very talented Caroline Poole. You can find more of Caroline's art at www.carolinepoole-artist.co.uk. I would also like to say a warm 'thank you' to Doreen and David Matthews for the fruitful exploration of their historical knowledge about the village of Kenton and our lovely 'Suffolk ways'. Last of all, I would like to acknowledge the considerable research undertaken by Elizabeth Barrett which I have constantly drawn on when writing about the village.

Melissa Nash has created an excellent period map of the Kenton district to complement both this book and the previous two novellas in the Winifred Smy series. It is free to download from the link below:

https://michaelheathauthor.com/genres/murder-mystery